MEASURE OF A MAN

BOOK YOUR PLACE ON OUR WEBSITE AND MAKE THE ARABESQUE ROMANCE CONNECTION!

We've created a customized website just for our very special Arabesque readers, where you can get the inside scoop on everything that's going on with Arabesque romance novels.

When you come online, you'll have the exciting opportunity to:

- View covers of upcoming books

- Learn about our future publishing schedule (listed by publication month and author)

- Find out when your favorite authors will be visiting a city near you

- Search for and order backlist books

- Check out author bios and background information

- Send e-mail to your favorite authors

- Join us in weekly chats with authors, readers and other guests

- Get writing guidelines

- AND MUCH MORE!

Visit our website at
http://www.arabesquebooks.com

MEASURE
of a MAN

Adrianne
Byrd

BET Publications, LLC
http://www.bet.com
http://www.arabesquebooks.com

ARABESQUE BOOKS are published by

BET Publications, LLC
c/o BET BOOKS
One BET Plaza
1900 W Place NE
Washington, DC 20018-1211

All Kensington Titles, Imprints and Distributed Lines are available at special quantity discounts for bulk purchases for sales promotions, premiums, fund-raising, and educational or institutional use. Special book excerpts or customized printings can also be created to fit specific needs. For details, write or phone the office of the Kensington special sales manager: Kensington Publishing Corp., 850 Third Avenue, New York, NY 10022. attn: Special Sales Department. Phone: 1-800-221-2647.

First Printing: January 2005
10 9 8 7 6 5 4 3 2 1

Printed in the United States of America

To Jasmine, Jordan, Jada, and Jackson
For being the best part of my day.

Chapter 1

For two hours, Local 1492 Dekalb Firefighters battled a three-alarm apartment blaze in the dead of night. December was a merciless month riddled with electrical fires. With this being their third call in the past twenty-four hours, the men of Local 1492 were pushed to the brink of exhaustion.

Firefighter Lincoln Carver ignored the pain pulsating through every muscle in his body as he hacked into a third-floor apartment. Despite the roar of the inferno surrounding him, he zeroed in on a series of coughs and cries for help on the other side of the door.

The moment the door gave way, black clouds of smoke enveloped him and obscured his vision. Operating purely on instinct, he strained his ears for any signs of life and heard none.

To his right, the walls glowed a dark black and orange with flames snaking toward him.

Someone is in here. You heard them.

Lincoln kept moving, convinced that his ears hadn't deceived him. Sweat poured around his face as his heart chugged the disappearing supply of oxygen.

Get out of here.

He shook off his inner command. Someone was still in there. He just knew it.

Behind him, a part of the roof caved in and burning debris missed him by mere inches.

It's too late. Get out!

Again, he shook off the warning. He just needed a few more seconds. However, Lincoln was out of time. Something cracked and then slammed into him.

"Has anyone seen Linc?" Flex Adams asked. He handed over a young girl covered in soot to one of the paramedics.

Omar Preston removed his hat and glanced around. "I thought he was with you."

Flex shook his head and surveyed the men around him. No Lincoln.

"I'm going back in," he announced and then felt a hand tug against his shoulder.

"If Linc is still in there—"

"Then I'll find him." Flex gave him a departing wink. "Be right back." He vaulted through the smoking door and up the fire-engulfed stairs without hesitation.

In times like these, Flex operated best on instinct. Too much thinking was a losing man's game and action saved lives. On the second floor, flames glowed across the carpet like a radiant liquid—a river of doom. Above him something creaked and then crashed, sending a shiver of fear coursing down his spine.

Where is he? He forced himself to remain calm. He started to enter an apartment, but thought better of it. *He's not in that one.*

The walls moaned around him as if the building

were alive. Next came the explosion of shattering windows and hunks of plaster fell around him. *Keep moving.* He flew up another flight of stairs, unsure if he was following the path to perdition.

Lincoln suppressed the pain in his lower back as he slid on his belly toward a little girl trembling in a corner. She sat with her knees drawn up against her chest, arms wrapped around her legs, while her eyes were wide with terror.

Her presence upped the ante. He had to make sure she made it out of there safe and sound. How he was going to do that was still unclear. As he approached, he guessed the child was about six years old. She was a pretty black girl with large doe-shaped eyes and hair parted down the center and fat plaits on each side. He could easily see the beautiful woman she would one day become.

Finally when he was within inches of her, her gaze withdrew from the flames licking up the walls to meet his eyes. But he saw no relief; if anything, her terror intensified.

Lincoln pulled himself up into a sitting position. He was surprised by the lack of pain in his back. In fact, he didn't feel anything.

"It's all right. I'm going to get you out of here," he shouted through the shield on his helmet.

The little girl covered her face with her hands and trembled uncontrollably.

Lincoln struggled to his feet and was careful as he swooped the child into his arms. However, the moment he took his first step, a sharp, hot pain boiled within him. When he stumbled, the girl's hands deserted her face and slid around his neck and choked off even more of his air supply.

He kept moving.

In his mind he was rushing, but it seemed as if it were taking forever to get out of the apartment. His heart pounded above the roar and crackle of the surrounding fire, so much so that he fleetingly wondered whether the over-active muscle was about to give out.

They had made it to the apartment's entrance when darkness encroached on the edges of his vision. In the building's hallway, flames blanketed the walls.

He kept moving.

A greasy sweat coated his face and dripped into his eyes as he headed toward the staircase. Suddenly, the child felt as if she weighed a ton and his legs threatened to buckle beneath him. He swore he heard shingles popping, rafters creaking, and windows exploding all around. They probably only had seconds before the ceiling caved in on them.

They weren't going to make it.

He was going to fail this beautiful little girl because the pain in his back and legs was unbearable now. As if sensing his surrender, the child tightened her hold and started to sob.

Don't give up. Keep moving.

Lincoln wasn't sure if those were his thoughts or if the child was transferring her own by a strange form of telepathy. Miraculously, he was still moving, but he felt dismally inadequate.

He heard a voice—a familiar one—calling his name. Out of the roiling smoke, a miracle appeared in full uniform. Before he could respond or react, a painful muscle spasm forced his legs to give up the fight.

They were falling.

* * *

Flex blinked back his shock, but managed to catch the brutal force of two falling bodies like a seasoned linebacker. After a few seconds of adjustment, he carried Lincoln over his shoulder and the child on his hip. Being a man with great strength and endurance, Flex trekked back down the stairs, dodging falling plaster, flaming bits of wood, and churning shrouds of black smoke.

In no time at all, Flex made good on his promise and returned to his men and the cold December night.

"Somebody get me a paramedic," he shouted and set the child down on the ground first.

"Ariel!"

"Nana!"

A woman raced forward and enfolded the child into her arms. "My beautiful baby. I thought I'd lost you forever."

Flex's heart warmed as he watched the scene from the corner of his eyes and lowered Lincoln's tall body onto the cold ground. Paramedics swarmed and took over his fallen brother's care.

He followed them until they loaded Lincoln into the ambulance and closed the door.

Fire Chief Harold Zahn pounded a heavy hand against Flex's back. "That was a pretty gutsy thing you did in there. You garnered a lot of respect from your new brothers."

Flex turned toward his superior's ruddy features with a lazy smile. "We all do what we can at L-1492, sir."

Chief Zahn's emerald gaze twinkled at him. "That might be true, but I have a feeling I'll be seeing great things from you."

"Thank you, sir. Your confidence is overwhelming."

"Well, it's sure going to be interesting around here

seeing how you just rescued the department's superman. He might wake up with a bruised ego. Be prepared."

Flex nodded. "Thanks for the warning."

Chapter 2

Peyton Garner joined three of her four older sisters at their usual hangout restaurant, the Peppermill. It was a nice cozy spot in the middle of San Jose and convenient to all of their jobs and homes. The two oldest, Sheldon and Frankie, were married; Michael, who was absent, was engaged; and the two youngest, Joey and Peyton, were single.

Actually, Peyton was newly divorced.

"I'm so sick of metrosexual men I could scream," Peyton said with a frustrated sigh. She jabbed her fork into her salad. "Just once I would like to date someone who knows something about cars other than how much they cost. Dennis and I were driving to Carmel last weekend and his car got a flat tire. This fool starts looking at me like I'm Rosie the Riveter or something."

Sheldon Casey, the oldest sister, leaned over and patted Peyton's arm. "Poor thing. What did you do?"

"I changed the damn flat. What else was I going to do?"

The girls snickered.

"It's not funny." Peyton lowered her fork and crossed

her arms. "I can't remember the last time I dated a man who knew how to get under the hood of a car without worrying about messing up his manicure, and that includes my ex-husband."

"I have to agree with Peyton," Joey piped in. "I think you two married the last of a dying breed."

"Oh, come on," Frankie cut in and waved her Harry Winston diamond wedding ring with a playful air. "There are plenty of good men out there."

"I'm not saying that a metrosexual man isn't a *good* man. I'm just saying that I can't tell the difference between dating them and dating women."

Sheldon laughed. "If you can't tell, then maybe the problem is *you*."

"Ha, ha." Peyton leaned back and crossed her arms. "Don't get me wrong, it's great that men can open up and talk about their 'feelings,' but they still need to know how to use a basic tool set. I'm tired of men who drink cappuccinos or fruity daiquiris. I want a scotch-on-the-rocks type of man."

Sheldon smiled. "And who takes his coffee—"

"Black." Peyton shrugged. "Okay, maybe sugar, but definitely no cream."

Her sisters erupted with laughter.

Peyton bobbed her head and rolled her hands to encourage her sisters to get it out of their systems. "Laugh if you want, but I want a manly man. Someone who knows how to repair the roof and install a toilet, for Pete's sake."

"Do you also want him to club you over the head and keep you barefoot and pregnant in the kitchen?" Sheldon admonished.

"You're a fine one to talk," Peyton snickered. "You've never worked a day in your life and when is baby number four due?"

"She has you there," Joey said.

Sheldon simply rolled her eyes, while her sisters laughed. "Hey, I can't help it if I'm fertile."

"Or that you two screw like rabbits," Frankie amended, and then held up her glass.

"Amen." Peyton and Joey clinked their glasses against Frankie's.

"I'm surrounded by haters." Sheldon laughed and refused to join them in their toast. "If a handyman is what you want, then why don't you just hang out at Home Depot and reel them in?"

"They're all married," Peyton and Joey said in unison, and then snickered.

"Okay, then there has to be a step that you two are missing," Frankie concluded.

"Tell me about it," Peyton said and took a sip of her drink. "You know the old saying that a man wants a lady on his arm and a freak in the bedroom?"

Her sisters nodded.

"Well, I still want a man who can pay for the house and fix it when it breaks down."

"I take it your ex didn't know how to install a toilet?"

"Please, Ricky didn't know how to screw in a lightbulb."

"I never knew what you saw in Ricky anyway. He was damn near forty and was still trying to be the next Tupac."

"It's hard trying to break into the music business," Peyton defended.

Sheldon's smile tightened. "The man needed a better backup plan than simply to marry a sugar mama."

Frankie and Joey sucked in a breath.

Peyton slowly inhaled and counted to ten before she responded. "I was not Ricky's sugar mama." The minute the words were out of her mouth, she felt foolish. Of course she was. She was married for three years and the man didn't have a job the entire time. She rolled her eyes. "Scratch that."

Her sisters laughed.

Frankie leaned over and wrapped a supportive arm around Peyton's shoulder. "You conquered the first step."

"Whatever. I might be the only divorcee in the family, but I tell you what, it certainly prepared me for what I *don't* want in a man."

Sheldon held up her glass. "Here's to Peyton finding the man of her dreams."

The girls lifted their glasses. "Hear! Hear!"

"You saved my life, man." Lincoln stretched out his hand to Flex from his hospital bed. "I owe you big time."

"Not bad for a new guy, eh?" Flex's meaty arm pumped Lincoln's hand with remarkable strength. "I heard you have to do rehab for a while. That sucks."

"Hey, if it means I don't have to run into burning buildings for a while, I'm all for it." Lincoln laughed and then winced in pain. "Enough about me, Mr. Hero. Omar was in here earlier showing me your mug shot splashed across the morning paper. Hell, they didn't even get my name spelled right."

Flex looked uncomfortable with the praise. "It's all in a day's work, right?"

"So true. I also heard you caught Chief Zahn's attention. That's not a small thing, buddy."

"Damn. Was the *National Enquirer* in here this morning?"

"News travels fast in the department."

"I see that," Flex said.

Lincoln smiled but had a hard time maintaining it. "How long you've been doing this?"

"I don't know." Flex lowered himself into a chair next to the bed. "Almost eight years."

"Most of those in California?"

"Yeah. My old man is the chief of my old precinct."

"Ah, following in the old man's footsteps?"

He nodded, but dropped his gaze.

Lincoln understood. "Me too. I'm a third-generation firefighter. Of course, I have a few uncles and cousins in the game, too. It's crazy."

Flex flashed him a noncommittal smile.

"Can I share something with you?" Lincoln asked and then made a quick glance over at the door.

"Sure."

He hesitated. Until now he'd never uttered the words he was about to say to anyone and they came with a high degree of guilt. "I'm thinking about hanging up my hat, man."

A frown hung on to Flex's broad features. "C'mon, Linc."

"Nah. I've been thinking about this way before last night. If anything, it just confirms my suspicions."

"Suspicions?"

Lincoln drew a breath and hated what he had to say. "I don't have it anymore. I've been doing this for eighteen years." He shook his head. "I'm tired of tasting soot and smelling smoke in my dreams. It's no way to live.

"It's not that I don't know the danger, I do. And for years I looked danger in the eye and laughed. I challenged it." He met his friend's gaze. "But lately, every fire seems to be calling my name."

Flex folded his arms and considered him. "I haven't known you long, but I never would've thought that *you* battled with fear."

"Don't you?"

"Yes, but not too many men would admit it."

Lincoln turned reflective and suddenly he wasn't

sure of anything. He loved his job. He'd dreamed of being a firefighter since he was a kid. So what was he talking about?

"Don't sweat it, Linc. You want this between us, then it will stay between us. But if you want my opinion, I don't think you mean any of this."

Lincoln nodded. "Yeah. You're right. I probably just got spooked."

"It's been known to happen. Ask any old-timer." Flex leaned back in his chair. "I know, it happened to me once."

"Really?" Lincoln considered him. "When?"

Flex shrugged. "A few months back. Just before my transfer went through. It was a pretty bad warehouse fire. I had the whole life-flashing-before-my-eyes thing happen. Hell, I'd forgotten I cheated on a third grade social studies test."

Lincoln laughed. "Well, I didn't quite experience that."

"Good. That must mean you can go into heaven with a clear conscience."

"Oh, I don't know about that." Lincoln shifted against his piles of pillows beneath him. His mind immediately rifled through the scores of women he'd dated. The relationships' inevitable doom was, more times than not, his fault. However, every lady in his past took a piece of his heart when she walked out of the door.

"I'll be damned. Are you blushing?"

Lincoln jerked from his thoughts, but then slid on a sly grin. "Women," he confessed. "I think they're the one thing I want to understand before the good Lord takes me out of here."

"Hell, I could help you there." Flex laughed. "I have so much estrogen flowing through my family that I suffer from PMS by default."

"Sisters?"

"Five of them."

Lincoln's eyes widened. "Damn, you aren't kidding. Any brothers?"

"Nope. I'm the baby."

Lincoln laughed as his gaze took in Flex's Herculean physique and had a hard time associating the word *baby* with him in any shape, form, or fashion. Just as quickly, Lincoln's active imagination slapped a wig, a dress, and some lipstick on his friend, and then multiplied the image by five. He was horrified by the results.

"So if you ever need help with women," Flex continued, "feel free to ask."

Lincoln shuddered. "Yeah, I'll do that."

"All right." Flex shrugged. "If you want to continue to crash and burn, that's your prerogative."

"If you're so knowledgeable, how come there isn't a ring around your finger?"

The smile vanished from Flex's lips as he glanced down at his bare finger.

Sensing that he'd struck a raw nerve, Lincoln immediately tried to make amends. "Hey, man. Sorry, I didn't mean to put my nose where it doesn't belong."

Flex waved off the apology and quickly returned the smile to his lips. "Nah, nah. It's all right. I mean, you had no way of knowing, but I was in a long-term relationship. Ten years to be exact."

"Really?" Lincoln crossed his arms in amazement. Other than the old-timers in the department, he couldn't think of one his buddies who had been in a relationship that long. Ten years might as well have been fifty years. "What happened?"

Flex shrugged. "I didn't listen to my sisters."

"Ah." Lincoln nodded. "They didn't like her?"

Flex's smile strained. "Something like that." He looked reflective before he spoke again. "There's a lot of good things about surviving in a family of women, and a lot of not so good things. One being subjected to five different opinions about everything."

Lincoln jumped in excitedly. "See? That's what I'm saying. I'm convinced that there are no two women alike. You go through one relationship, trying to incorporate what you've learned during the last relationship, and that woman turns out to be the total opposite of the last girl. I had this one woman dump me because I built this big mahogany bookcase instead of buying her jewelry for her birthday. It's maddening. Which means more—something you just pick out in a store or something that took you six weeks to build?"

Flex's laugh returned. "You are lost, huh?"

"Lost? Hell, I'm just about ready to give up."

"Don't tell me that you're going to swing the other way."

"Ooh, no." Lincoln rolled his eyes. "I'm one hundred percent a ladies' man, but I might have to give up the notion of settling down. It seems the harder I try, the worse things turn out."

"I guess that goes to prove that you could never judge a book by its cover." Flex swept a hand toward him. "Looking at you, I would never have thought you had trouble attracting women."

"Whoa, whoa." Lincoln held up his hands. "I never said that I had trouble attracting women. It's the right woman I'm talking about. Women say that they want a nice guy, but the minute they meet one, suddenly they want a thug. It's crazy."

"Maybe you're trying too hard."

He thought it over for a moment. "You think so?"

"Could be." Flex shrugged. "I mean, what's the rush anyway? How old are you?"

"Thirty-nine."

"There you go. Warren Beatty didn't hang up his

playa shoes until he was staring down the barrel at sixty. Besides, my sister Peyton always says that she can sense desperation in a man."

"Really?" Lincoln frowned. "Wait a minute. Your sister's name is Peyton?"

Flex rolled his eyes. "I have a Sheldon, Frankie, Michael, Joey, and a Peyton." He shrugged. "My father kept hoping for a boy."

"And when he finally got one, he named you Flex?"

"Not exactly." Flex shifted in his chair. "Flex is sort of a nickname I gave myself when I was a wrestler in high school."

"Mind if I ask?"

He hesitated.

"I promise, it won't leave this room." Lincoln crossed his heart. "If you want to know the truth, Lincoln isn't my name either."

"Really?"

"Nope. It's Trey Carver; my friends dubbed me Lincoln." He shrugged. "When I was fifteen I snuck out of the house and took my father's brand-new Lincoln for a cruise around the neighborhood. Problem was, it never made it back home."

Flex winched. "You wrecked it?"

Lincoln nodded. "Wrapped it around a pole and knocked out all the electricity in the neighborhood. When my father was through with me, I couldn't sit down for a week. From that day forth my friends called me Lincoln. It started off as a joke, but it stuck." He glanced back at his friend. "So spill it. What's your real name?"

Flex huffed and then mumbled. "It's Francis. Francis Marion Adams."

Chapter 3

Peyton rushed through the door of her apartment ready to pass out from the pain in her feet from wearing her brand-new Prada shoes. Sprinting to the living room, she collapsed on her plush cream and gold sofa, and not a minute too soon.

"I love you, but you have got to go." She peeled her babies off and sighed with relief as blood rushed back into her toes. However, that was the high cost of beauty.

The phone rang and she moaned in disgust before she reached over and picked up the cordless from the end table. "Hello."

"Hey, Peyton, it's me."

"Me who?" she asked, frowning. All the women in the family tended to sound alike.

"Me, Michael." Her sister had the nerve to be annoyed. "Have you talked to Flex today?"

"Can't say that I have. Why?"

"Well, I was on the Web today and I ran across his picture on a news site."

Concern squeezed Peyton's heart. "Is he all right? Did something happen?"

"Yes and yes. According to the papers he's fine, but he's being hailed as a hero for saving a little girl and one of his colleagues from an apartment fire. Can you believe it?"

"Really?" Peyton's shoulders slumped with relief, but she pulled herself up and limped all the way to her home office. "He's been in Atlanta for three months and he's already a hero. That's fantastic."

"Dad is going to be thrilled when I tell him. Who knows? It might even salve some of the hurt feelings he has over Flex transferring to another state."

Peyton booted up her computer. "I'm surprised you didn't call him first."

"I tried, but it's poker night."

"Shame on you. How could you ever forget that?" Peyton teased, and in no time she was surfing the Web. She found an article with a picture of her brother smiling and her heart swelled with pride. "I sure do miss him," she said, forgetting that she still had the phone tucked under her ear.

"I know what you mean. We should plan a trip to go out and see him."

"What, the whole family?"

"If not, at least a few of us. Heck, we could go in turns. That's the best way to keep an eye on him."

Peyton shook her head as she pressed her print button. "I seem to remember him saying that he wanted to get away from our constant nosying."

"Whose nosying?" Michael's voice rose an octave. "We're just checking on him. Besides, Flex needs to learn that it's not healthy to run away from his problems."

"He's not running. He just needs a break."

"From us or from Morgan?"

"Look, just because their relationship ended—"

"Cut me a break, Peyton. You're starting to sound like Flex's parrot instead of one of us. Put the pieces together. He asked for that transfer within days of their breakup."

"Well, they were together for ten years."

"So he moves away. He hardly calls any of us and for the first time in his entire life he won't be with the family for Christmas. Someone should go and be with him. I don't like the idea of him being alone for the holidays."

Peyton frowned. She hadn't really thought about this apparently as much as Michael had. "Maybe you're right."

"Of course I'm right. So why don't you go?"

Peyton nearly choked. "What? Why me?"

"What, you're not concerned anymore?"

"Well, sure I am, but—"

"But nothing. You and Joey are the most flexible. Neither of you is married—"

"Neither are you."

"Don't be silly. I'm engaged. It's the same as being married. I tell you, you should consider yourself lucky. You don't have to juggle trying to see two different families anymore."

Peyton rolled her eyes, but didn't have the heart to remind Michael that she'd been *engaged* for nearly four years now. "Then Joey should go. I have way too much work to do during the holidays. Three of my artists are having major shows in January. No way I can just pick up and travel to the other side of the country right now."

"Sure you can. You and Joey should both go. Frankie and I could probably go in the spring and we can give Sheldon and her husband the honor of going in the summer."

"You've already talked this over with them, haven't you?"

A long pause hung on the phone line before Peyton rolled her eyes and leaned back in her chair.

"You know how much I hate it when you plan things behind my back."

"Oh, chill out. No need to get your panties in a bunch. Either you want to do this or you don't."

"Thanks for asking—I don't. I mean, what if Flex doesn't want me there?"

"That's a very good point," Michael conceded.

"Thank you."

"Which is why we're not going to tell him."

A red flag flashed before Peyton's eyes. "Whoa. Bad idea. If he gets mad about my sudden appearance, then I'll be the one he'll take it out on. No, I say this is your idea and you should go. I'll take spring duty with Frankie."

"Peyton—"

"Michael," she snapped back in the same impatient tone. "We need to let Flex live his own life. If he doesn't want to come home for Christmas, then we need to respect that."

"Flex doesn't know how to ask for help. You know that. He's too busy acting like nothing ever bothers him. This Morgan thing has really crushed him and I'm surprised that you're buying in to his denial act."

Peyton sighed, but she did believe that Flex ran to Atlanta to get away from the pain of ending a long relationship. Maybe he shouldn't be alone for the holidays. Hadn't she heard somewhere that the suicide rate skyrocketed around these times?

"I tell you what. I'll call him and get a feel for his state of mind. If I sense that he's lonely or miserable, then I'll go. If not, then I think we should respect his wishes."

Her sister didn't respond.

"Take it or leave it, Michael."

"Fine. I'll take it. But dig deep, Peyton. He always has been able to pull the wool over your eyes."

"Fine."

"Call me back and tell me everything he says."

"Michael—"

"That's the condition," Michael insisted.

"All right. You have a deal," Peyton finally agreed.

Lincoln tried everything he could to reach the ungodly itch that was in the center of his plastered leg, but nothing was working. He thought about buzzing a nurse and begging her for a coat hanger of some kind, yet in the end he figured he would come across as being a baby about the whole thing.

Just don't think about it, he told himself, and tried to lie still.

"Is the leg still killing you?" Flex asked, returning to his room and carrying two sodas. He handed one over to Lincoln. "Sorry, but the vending machine doesn't carry Heineken."

"Thanks." Lincoln accepted the can and set it down on the desk beside his bed. "You wouldn't happen to have a coat hanger on you, would you?"

"I knew I forgot to bring something." Flex laughed. "Hey, you mind if I hit the can before I head out?"

"Nah, knock yourself out." He wiggled a finger into his cast, certain that this time he was going to reach his itch.

Flex just shook his head at Lincoln's antics and stepped into his bathroom. No sooner had he closed the door when a shrill ring filled the room.

Lincoln looked over at the table and spotted Flex's cell phone. "Hey, it's your phone, Francis."

"Not funny," Flex called out. "Can you answer it? I'm expecting a call from my landlady."

"No problem." Lincoln leaned over onto his side and picked up the phone. "Yellow," he greeted with more chirpiness than he felt.

Silence greeted him.

He tried again. "Hello."

A female's lyrical voice came onto the line. "Hello, Flex?"

"No, actually I'm, uh, a friend of Flex's." Lincoln glanced over at the bathroom door. "Flex is, uh, sort of indisposed at the moment. Can I take a message?"

"A *friend* of Flex's?" the woman asked.

Lincoln frowned. "Yes, I am. Are you the landlady?"

"Oh no." The woman suddenly sounded excited. "I'm Peyton, Flex's sister."

"Ah, Peyton. Yes, your brother told me about you." He smiled, quite taken with the sound of the woman's voice. "Yeah, he told me all about . . . let's see, uh, Sheldon, Frankie, Michael, Joey, and Peyton. Am I right?"

"Wow. That's pretty good." She laughed. "Well, this is great. He's moved to Atlanta and has already met a new . . . friend."

Lincoln laughed. "I'm sure I'm not the only one. A man like your brother won't have any trouble in that department."

"Yeah, he's quite a guy." Her voice sounded full of pride. "You like him?"

"Like him? Hell, after last night, he could never do any wrong by me."

"Oh, that's great. The girls will be happy to hear that he's . . . moved on." She sighed and he could hear her relax. "We were sort of worried when he left. He had just, uh—"

"Oh, the bad relationship thing." Lincoln nodded. "Yeah, he told me all about it."

"He told you?"

"Yeah, ten years," Lincoln shook his head. "It's a shame, but you know he seems like he's ready to get his feet wet again. I'm just the person to push him along."

"This is great." She laughed. "And here my sisters

were trying to convince me to fly out and surprise him for Christmas."

"Well, you should." Lincoln sat up. "I would love to meet some of his family." Peyton in particular, he thought. From the bathroom, he heard the toilet flush and then the sudden spray of water from the sink.

"You would? You don't think Flex would mind?"

"Why should he? He has had nothing but good things to say to me about you girls."

"That's good to know. I have to see if I can work it into my schedule, but if I don't come this month I'm sure I'll make it there in the near future."

"Sounds good."

"Great, er, hmm, I'm sorry. I didn't catch your name."

"It's Trey, but my friends call me—"

"Trey. Hmm, that's a nice name. Well, it's been good talking with you. Hopefully, I'll see you soon."

"You got it."

The bathroom door opened and Lincoln disconnected the call.

"Who was it?" Flex asked.

Lincoln tossed him the phone and gave him a wide smile. "It was a wrong number."

Peyton jumped to her feet and performed a victory dance, despite her sore feet, in the middle of the room before she called her sister Michael.

"You'll never guess who I just talked to," she squealed.

Michael's voice perked with excitement. "Who?"

"Flex's new *boyfriend.*"

Chapter 4

"What?" Michael's voice leaped a few octaves. "He already has a new boyfriend? Are you sure?"

"A man answered his cell phone and introduced himself as Flex's new *friend*." Peyton plopped back onto her sofa. "And that's not all. He sounded sexy as hell."

"Now that's funny. Our baby brother's been back on the market a couple of months and he's able to find a man before you."

"Ha, ha, ha." Peyton rolled her eyes at the barb. "This is a good sign, don't you think?"

"I don't know. It's sort of soon, don't you think? What else did the guy say?"

Peyton tried to recall the conversation. "He said that Flex could do no wrong and that he knew all about us—oh, he also knew about Morgan."

"Flex told him about Morgan?"

"Yeah. This is great news, we need to get the other girls on the phone."

"I agree."

After performing a series of conference calls, all the sisters were on the phone. Peyton quickly told them about her conversation with Trey and the line was abuzz with squeals and laughter.

"Do you think he knew this guy before he left California?" Sheldon asked. "I mean, it's sort of fast, don't you think? Flex isn't the type to move so quickly."

"You know, I was just thinking the same thing," Frankie cut in. "It would make sense if he knew this guy before he left."

"And how would he have met him before he left?" Joey asked.

"There's all sorts of ways," Sheldon said with strained patience. "Oh, what if he'd met him on line. I hear the Internet is the new singles bar of the millennium."

"An Internet hookup?" Peyton drummed her fingers against her lips. "I met someone once online."

"When?" Four voices replied in unison.

Why did she open her big mouth? "It was a few months ago. We only met for drinks. No big deal."

"No big deal? What happened?" Michael demanded.

"Nothing. The guy was a total loser. He weighed about a hundred pounds more than he said, he wore a bad toupee, and he still lived at home with his mother."

The girls gasped, and then filled the line with, "You poor thing," and, "He could have been a mass murderer."

"It was just that one time," Peyton reminded them. "But I tell you, this Trey guy sounded hot. I mean, he had this deep, smooth baritone going on. If he's half as good looking as he sounds, Flex has to be in hog heaven."

"I think we should find out more about this guy," Frankie interjected. "The idea of Flex meeting some stranger on the Internet and uprooting his whole life to be with this man isn't setting too well with me."

"I have to agree," Sheldon chimed in. "This doesn't sound like Flex. He hasn't so much as hinted that there was someone new in his life."

"Then why would this guy be answering his cell phone?" Peyton asked. "And when I asked him if he liked Flex, he said that after last night, Flex could do no wrong."

"Sounds like a love connection to me," Joey agreed. "I'm happy for him. He deserves it after that creep Morgan."

"I thought he was putting out a fire last night," Michael said.

"That was early this morning or maybe this guy likes dating someone who gets their name in the paper. How should I know?"

"I still think someone should go there and check this dude out," Michael insisted.

"I'm going," Peyton said. "Trey invited me down. He claimed that he wanted to meet some of Flex's family."

"Trey," Frankie repeated. "I don't know if I like that name. It sounds—slick. He isn't a playa, is he?"

"Seems like I heard that name recently," Michael mused.

Peyton rolled her eyes. "I like it. It sounds sexy."

"The article," Michael said. "Wasn't Trey something or another the name of the other firefighter Flex rescued?"

Peyton rushed over to the article she'd printed. Her eyes scanned down the page and until she read the name. "You're right. It says so right here that 'Firefighter Flex Adams raced back into the burning apartment building in search of his missing colleague and returned within minutes with Fire

Lieutenant Trey Carver draped over his shoulder
and six-year-old Ariel Porter in his arms. When asked
why he risked his life after everyone had cleared out
of the building, Mr. Adams smiled and said that
"Lieutenant Carver is important to me and the men
at Local 1492. I would risk my life for him any day of
the week." ' "

Peyton and her sisters sighed, "Oh, how romantic."

"What do you mean it was the wrong number?"
Flex said, flipping open his phone. "I heard you in
here talking."

Lincoln smiled.

Flex read the name of his last caller from his cell's
screen ID. "Peyton called?"

"Damn technology." Lincoln laughed. "Yeah, she
called, and if you don't mind me saying, she sounds
pretty hot. Is she dating anybody?"

"I thought we agreed that you weren't jumping
back into the dating scene so soon."

"Did I say that?" Lincoln frowned. "I don't remember that."

Flex just laughed and walked around the empty
chair to grab his leather jacket. "I'm heading out.
You make sure you take care of yourself and try not
to drive the nurses crazy."

"Ah, you're going to leave me hangin' like that? I
wanted to know some more about your sister."

"Forget about it," Flex said, heading to the door.
"If you date one sister, then you're dating all five of
them. Trust me, you're not ready for that kind of ag-
gravation."

"Hey!"

"Catch you later." Flex waved and then left the room.

"Fine. Be that way, *Francis!*" Lincoln laughed and

then fell back on the bed pillows. But within seconds the itch on his leg grew worse and he had to finally call a nurse for help.

Never being a television sort of person, Lincoln quickly grew restless. It was hours after he finished his hospital dinner when his best friend, Tyrone Ellis, finally paid him a visit.

"Hey, Dog. I thought that you would never get here."

"What can I say? I had to come and check on my boy, right?" Tyrone's face lit up as the men's hands slapped together. "I have to admit I thought I'd never see this day. Badass Lincoln Carver, a man able to leap burning buildings in a single bound, is laid up in the hospital."

"Yeah, me too. Guess I'm going to have to retire my blue tights, huh?"

Tyrone, a short man of five-two, slid into the empty chair beside Lincoln's bed. "I read what happened in the newspaper, *Carver*. I don't know how you continue to eat smoke for a living, but—"

"Since when is being a cop a safer job?" Flex cut him off before his friend could get going. "How many times have you been shot at this year?"

"Are we including the shots fired by my ex-girl?"

Lincoln shook his head. "Face it. There's something wrong with both of us."

"You might have a point there." Tyrone leaned back in his chair and looked his friend over. "So who's the dude that pulled you out?"

"New guy. Name is Flex Adams. Don't know too much about him, but he seems like a decent guy. I'm thinking about asking him to join us and the guys next Thursday."

"A new inductee to poker night? Wow, this guy must have made some impression on you. We haven't had a new guy since our days at Morehouse."

"He saved my ass. As far as I'm concerned you can't make a better impression."

"Good point. I'll let the guys know."

"Plus," Lincoln added, "I have another agenda."

Tyrone's brows rose inquisitively. "A woman?"

Lincoln nodded. "You know me so well."

Flex entered his apartment, happy to be home for the next forty-eight hours. The first thing he wanted to do was call his family—let them know how he was doing; however, a part of him wasn't up for the task.

He loved his family. Truly, he did, but being the youngest of six children came with a heavy price. His career moves, financial decisions, and personal relationships were all open for discussion at family meetings and gatherings. Everyone, in their own *loving* way, had an opinion about what was going on in his life.

Which was why, when he decided to move two thousand miles away from his family, the grumbling was probably heard clear over in China. Though his family was one variable in the equation—ending a ten-year relationship was the other.

"Everyone needs a fresh start," he mumbled and headed toward the kitchen. No sooner had he grabbed a beer than his phone rang. Undoubtedly, it was one of his sisters. He reentered the living room to hear his answering machine tell the caller to leave a message at the beep.

"Flex, it's me—Morgan. If you're there, pick up."

Flex froze in the center of the room.

"Well, I just read an article about you and I was worried. When you get this message, please give me a call. All right. Bye."

Minutes passed before Flex shook off his stupor and took a swig from his beer; however, it wasn't enough to dull his senses, so he drained the bottle with one long chug. When that didn't help, he decided to stay busy by hanging the rest of his pictures up on the wall. But no matter what he did, Morgan's voice floated through his mind. *How did he get this number? What makes him think I want to talk to him?*

Flex took a shower and then grabbed another beer. And still he was obsessed over Morgan. He kept drinking while his thoughts chased each other. Though Flex considered himself a strong man, physical strength failed to give him the tools to handle emotional abuse—and Morgan Ramsey wrote the book on head games.

When the room began to spin, Flex collapsed onto his monstrous king-size bed. As he floated in an emotional stupor, he had a sudden urge to talk to someone—someone who understood better than anyone.

"Hello."

"Hey, P.J., it's me. Did I call at a bad time?"

Peyton rolled over in bed and glanced at her clock. "Isn't it two in the morning there?"

"I don't know. I-I can't sleep."

She frowned at his slurred words and she sat up. "Is something wrong?"

"No, no. It's nothing like that. I . . . just—just." He sighed. "I miss talking to you, that's all."

Peyton knew something was definitely wrong. "You know I miss you around here. Sunday dinner hasn't been the same since you left. Not to mention Dad—well, we all miss you."

"How is Dad doing?"

"He's a little hurt, but you know he loves you, don't you?"

"Is that what he said?"

"Do any of us have to say it?" she asked gently. "But maybe you . . . we shouldn't have kept your secret for so long. I mean, I think he feels foolish for being the only one who didn't know. That's all."

A long pause hung over the line before Flex responded. "Maybe he just didn't want to know."

"Perhaps you didn't *want* to tell him," she said, and then waited through another long silence. Peyton liked to think that her relationship with her brother was good. Especially since they were the last two in the clan. She tried her best not to fuss over him or put her nose where it didn't belong. Mainly because she hated it when her sisters pried into her life. However, there were times, like now, when she wanted nothing more than to rattle the truth out of Flex. Why did he feel like he had to run from the family, and why so far?

"If there's something really troubling you, you can talk to me," she said, and then held her breath.

"I know," he said, but there had been a slight pause before he answered.

She held the phone and listened to him breathe. Had there been a fight between him and this new guy? Or worse, had this Trey character told Flex that she was planning a surprise visit and he was trying to figure out a way to tell her not to come?

"Morgan called here tonight," he finally said.

Peyton released the air pinned in her lungs. "Did you talk to him?"

"I don't have anything to say."

At the pain in her brother's voice, she wanted to fold him in her arms. "He's a jerk. Don't let him get to you. Joey said that she saw him and his new boyfriend at the mall last week. Morgan went out of his way to stop her and ask how you were doing."

"Did she give him this number?" Flex snapped.

"I don't know. I don't think that she would—"

"Great. He probably thinks I left California with my tail tucked between my legs. Well, I've moved on.

You make sure you tell him that the next time you see him."

"I will, I will," she said, trying to placate him, while also trying to remove her foot from her mouth.

"Yeah. And you tell him that my new man is ten times better looking than him."

"Got it. I'll make him green with envy," Peyton promised, and then decided to tread on shaky ground. "You know, you didn't tell me that you had a new boyfriend."

"Huh?" Flex's voice dropped. "Yeah, well, I do. And he's the best thing that could ever have happened to me."

"Well, that's great," Peyton encouraged. "I'm happy for you. Who is he? When did you meet him?"

"Huh? Oh, well, I, uh, met him here in Atlanta—at a club. He's really a great guy."

Peyton frowned again. She was certain her brother was more than a little tipsy. "I still think it's wonderful. What's his name?"

"His name?"

She laughed. "He does have a name, doesn't he?"

"Of course he does. It's, uh, T-Trey. Yeah, Trey— great guy. You'd love him."

Peyton smiled against the phone. "I love him already."

Chapter 5

After spending more than twenty-four hours in the hospital, Lincoln was more than ready to go home. As he glanced out the window of his room at a beautiful Saturday morning, his mind filled with all the things he'd rather be doing—for instance, finishing his latest sculpture.

He sighed. The one thing not too many people knew about Trey "Lincoln" Carver was that he was a closet artist. He had been bending and sculpting metal as a hobby for nearly twenty years. He didn't know whether he was any good or not, but it definitely had a way of relaxing him.

All of his life he loved to take things apart and put them together again. But sometime in his freshman year at college, he not only took things apart, he started to assemble them differently. It was fun—no, therapeutic—changing things, creating things.

Once, he had made the mistake of showing his father one of his creations. "What the hell is it?" his father had thundered, and then erupted into laughter.

"I don't know. It's an abstract." Lincoln remembered wringing his hands. "I got some parts down at old man Cullers's junkyard."

"It looks like something from the junkyard." His father's hard but amused gaze turned toward him. "Is this something they're teaching you down at that expensive college: how to turn junk into more junk?"

Lincoln blinked the painful memory away and swallowed a lump in his throat. No matter how many times he told himself that his father hadn't meant to hurt him that day, he never got over it.

After his morning breakfast, his longtime friends and poker buddies, Henry, Desmond, and Walter, showed up.

"I was wondering when you knuckleheads were going to get here.

Desmond snapped a picture of Lincoln propped up in bed. "You know we wouldn't have missed this Kodak moment for anything in the world." He laughed. "How the nurses been treating you in here? Have you had a sponge bath yet?"

The men laughed as Lincoln responded, "Get your mind out of the gutter."

"Hell, that's the least they can do for the bill you're about to get for being in this mutha," Desmond said and scratched his bald and weirdly shaped head. "Am I right?"

Walter frowned and pressed his wire-rimmed glasses to his face. "Don't pay him any mind."

"When have I ever?" Lincoln asked.

"How are they treating you?" Henry asked.

"I can't complain."

"What happened?" his friends asked in unison.

Lincoln shrugged as he condensed yesterday's events. "Seems a beam fell and shattered my ankle. They put a metal plate in my ankle and promised me

I should be as good as new in a few months." He ended with a smile.

The group's expressions looked crushed with disappointment.

"What does that mean for your firefighting career?" Walter asked sternly. He was an M.D. himself—actually, a gynecologist, which was the best kind of doctor, according to his friends.

"I don't know yet. I'm trying not to think about it."

"It wouldn't be so bad if you took a desk job, would it?" Henry inquired. Being a paper pusher himself at the mayor's office, he couldn't see anything wrong with that.

"I don't know if I'm cut out for that kind of work," Lincoln admitted, but realized that his life was quickly approaching a crossroad. Admittedly, he was nervous about returning to a job that was proving more difficult as the years rolled by. But at the same time, it was all he knew.

Desmond perked up. "Don't worry about it. I'm sure you'll be racing into another fire in no time. Granted, I don't know why any sane person would want to do that, but who am I to judge?"

A knock drew everyone's attention to the door.

Flex strolled inside with a wide grin, but Lincoln's gaze fell to the bag from Burger King. "Please tell me that's not what I think it is."

"I figured you might want some real food," Flex said.

"Boys," Lincoln announced. "I'd like you to meet the man who saved my life—Flex Adams."

Flex set the food down on the table and shook hands with the gang as Lincoln introduced them one by one.

"The mayor's chief of staff?" Flex asked, pumping Henry's hands. "That has to be an interesting job."

Henry's chest puffed up with pride. "Well, I don't want to brag."

"Of course he does," Desmond cut in. "It's what he does best."

"You know, Desmond works for the city as well." Henry slid his hand into his pockets. "Trash collection."

Unbelievably, Desmond's midnight complexion darkened. "It's a decent living, you—"

"All right, guys," Lincoln snapped, and rubbed his pulsing temples. "Let's not fight today. This is a hospital, after all."

Flex looked like he didn't know whether to laugh or run.

"Don't worry," Lincoln said, unwrapping his Whopper. "They're like this all the time. You get used to it." He held up his sandwich. "Good looking out."

"Don't mention it. So when are you heading home?" Flex asked.

"I'm going to try and make a prison break today. I have to get out of this bed."

"Wow. The crowd's all here," Tyrone said, bursting into the room and carrying Lincoln's leather gym bag.

Another round of handshakes and high fives ensued while Lincoln chomped on his burger. So far, it looked like everyone was getting along—except for Henry and Desmond.

"Linc tells us that you're going to be our new buddy on poker night," Tyrone said.

"Oh?" Flex looked over at Lincoln.

"Actually, bigmouth," Lincoln admonished, "I haven't asked him yet." He met Flex's stare. "Do you play?"

"I might be a little rusty. When do you guys get together?"

"Thursdays. Of course, you being new at the department, you might not be able to get every Thursday off, but you're more than welcome to join us any time."

Flex's smile broadened. "Thanks, I just might take you up on that."

"That burger is looking pretty good," Walter commented, and then his stomach growled to second the motion. "I'm going to head out and grab me something."

"Hey, I'm coming with you," Desmond said.

"I skipped breakfast," Henry added.

Before Lincoln knew it, his three stooges left with promises to return later.

"Seems like a nice bunch of guys," Flex said, crossing his arms. "How long have you all known each other?"

"Too damn long," Tyrone answered for Lincoln. "By the way, I swung by your house and picked up a change of clothes."

"Thanks, dog."

Tyrone frowned and crossed his arms. "Mind if I ask what is all that metal stuff in your spare room?"

Lincoln stopped stuffing his mouth and cast a nervous glance around the room. "What?"

"Those statues. Are you working on something?"

Lincoln's brain scrambled for an answer while he washed what he had in his mouth down with a swig of Coke.

"It actually looked pretty cool," Tyrone added.

Stunned, Lincoln felt as if his brain had completely shut down. "You, uh, liked it?"

"Yeah." Tyrone bobbed his head. "You sure have a lot of them in there."

"You should see the attic and the garage."

Tyrone shrugged and then reached for one of Lincoln's onion rings. "So what are they?"

"Sculptures," he decided to go with the truth. "I've been working on them for a little while."

"A little while? It looked like a small warehouse in there."

"You *really* liked them?" Lincoln smiled.

"From what I saw they looked pretty cool. I never knew you were into that kind of thing. You ought to try and sell some of them."

"Sell them?" He laughed, but was intrigued by the thought as well. "Who would want that junk?"

"My sister always quotes that one man's trash is another man's treasure," Flex jumped into the conversation. "Besides, have you seen what they called art nowadays?"

A fusion of emotions assaulted Lincoln, but he was riding high over the fact that Tyrone actually *liked* his stuff. "I'll look into it," Lincoln announced. "Who knows? Maybe this is the beginning of a whole new chapter for me."

Christmas came and went and Peyton was unable to make it to Atlanta. However, she did jet around the country for one art show after another. Working with museums and art dealers was a breeze. It was working with *artists* that usually drove her crazy.

Her latest protégée, Kanji, was a brilliant painter and a brilliant pain in the ass. According to her, nothing was ever right—from hotel rooms to the kinds of questions that critics asked. But the paychecks kept a smile on Peyton's face and an extra bounce in her step.

Now it was the first day of spring and the first time she'd been in her office in San Jose since Valentine's Day. *Valentine's Day.* She rolled her eyes from just thinking about the crappy holiday.

"Peyton," Basil Rollé said, jumping up from behind Peyton's desk. "I thought you weren't coming back until tomorrow."

"I can see that." Peyton smiled as she entered the room. "Getting a little too comfortable around here, are you?"

Basil's high-yellow complexion burned red from embarrassment. "Sorry about that. It's just so much nicer in here," she offered as an excuse.

"I know. That's why *I* chose it." She laughed and settled into her chair. And as if she had a Lojack on her butt the phone rang.

"Before you answer it, Kanji called twice this morning. She wants to come home."

"She just left for Tokyo yesterday."

"She says she's homesick." Basil folded her arms and forced a tight smile. "So, needless to say, Tae Zhao, the art director at the Meguro Museum of Art, has also phoned."

The call went to voice mail.

Peyton drew a breath and popped the top off her grande cappuccino. "Kanji is giving me gray hair."

"Cornel Dyson has also been calling. He said that he couldn't reach you on your cell."

"Dyson, really?" A faint smile hugged her lips at the thought of the ruggedly handsome . . . and married man.

"I know what you mean." Basil sighed with an equally wide smile. "All the good ones are taken."

"And a lot of the bad ones," Peyton added with a wink and picked up the phone. By the second ring, Cornel Dyson's whiskeylike voice filled the phone line.

"Ah, P.J. Garner. What a breath of fresh air," he praised.

Peyton eased back in her chair and crossed her legs. "Mr. Dyson, I could say the same for you. I heard you've been looking for me."

"Yes, I have. It's been about a week now. I take it the job is keeping you busy?"

"Unfortunately. But hey, it pays the bills."

"That it does." He snickered. "I called you because I have a referral for you. I mean, if you're taking on new clients."

"A referral from the great Cornel? Mind if I ask why you're not taking this artist on?"

"I'd like to, but I really am working with a full roster."

Peyton took a sip of her coffee. Dyson had been her mentor in the business from day one. He represented the best of the best, and as far as she knew he was pretty stingy with his talent, so she didn't really know what to make of a referral. If this person was Dyson quality, he would undoubtedly give up sleep to fit the person into his lineup.

"I don't know, Cornel," she said, hedging. "Things are pretty busy around here, too."

"Hey, no pressure. Do you think you can at least squeeze in a meeting? You can just check out his portfolio and see if you like him."

She drew a deep breath and reached into her purse for her Palm Pilot. "When are we talking about?"

"It's up to you, but I do have to tell you this guy is on the East Coast."

"He knows how to hop a plane, doesn't he?"

Dyson laughed. "Most likely."

Peyton stared at her crammed calendar. "It's not looking good. I'm packed all week and then I leave for New York on Friday. I have a show to attend on Saturday and then I'm on vacation for two weeks to visit my brother."

"How about he meets you in New York?"

Peyton's brows rose in surprise. "Does he live there?"

"No, but I can make sure he gets there to meet with you. Are you interested?"

Peyton sensed his determination. Maybe she should

check this person out. "What the hell?" she finally said, and reached for a pen. "What's the artist's name?"

"Carver," Dyson said. "Lincoln Carver."

Chapter 6

Peyton and Joey arrived in New York tired and irritable. After having survived airport security, crying babies, and horrible airline food, all Peyton wanted to do was to sink into a nice warm bed. However, their nightmare of a trip wasn't over yet.

Joey's luggage arrived okay, but Delta had no clue as to what part of the world Peyton's new Louis Vuitton bags were headed.

And still, it wasn't over.

The women piled into the first available taxi, and ended up with a driver whose English was highly suspect. He drove in circles through downtown New York pretending, in Peyton's opinion, not to know where their hotel was located.

Peyton glanced at the meter and performed a double take when she read seventy-two dollars. "We're not paying you to be lost, Kareem," Peyton thundered, catching on to the man's game. "We're not paying you any more than thirty dollars for this ride and we're not getting out until you get us there."

Fifteen minutes later, the cab stopped in front of the New York Palace.

"Sheesh. He was nothing but a crook," Joey said, storming away from the cab.

Peyton rolled her eyes. "I wonder how many people actually fall for that stunt."

"I hate to admit it, but I probably would have if you weren't here."

Peyton shivered when a breeze whipped across her body. She tugged her coat tight and waited for the doorman to allow them entry.

"I'm ready to change out of these clothes and hit the clubs," Joey announced.

"You have to be kidding me," Peyton said, moaning. "I want to go to sleep."

"I heard the nightlife in this town is off the chain. We have to at least check out 2i's."

"Girl, my feet are killing me and I don't have anything to wear. Did you forget, the airline lost my luggage?" Peyton stopped at the check-in counter.

A few minutes later, the girls walked into their beautiful room overlooking the city. As promised, Peyton dove for the nearest bed.

"No, no, no." Joey rushed over to her and tried to pull her off the bed. "I want to go dancing. You promised me before we came."

"Go away."

"C'mon, it's Friday night *and* it's New York," she whined. "Who knows? We might even meet P.Diddy or somebody. We could end up at his place swimming in a bed of money."

Peyton tugged her arm back and rolled her eyes. "You have one hell of an imagination." She sat up. "Besides, thanks to the friendly skies I don't have anything to wear. I have to find time to go shopping before we head out to Atlanta on Monday."

"You know better than that." Joey turned from the bed to grab her bags. "You can wear something of mine. Oh, what about that short silver number I bought just before we left?"

"You mean those two strips of fabric? No, thanks. I'll catch pneumonia and blow my meeting with this Carver dude."

"Work, work, work. That's all you ever think of. No wonder you meet the same type of men. Stiff business suits or oversensitive artsy-fartsy men."

"Just give me the damn outfit. Anything will be better than listening to your hollow words of wisdom." Peyton stood up from the bed.

"Hollow?"

Peyton lifted her sister's right hand. "I don't see any rings on your finger."

"I could've been married by now if I wanted to," Joey said, lifting her chin. "Ryan Mendes asked me to marry him once."

"Yeah, back when you two were in grade school."

"A proposal is a proposal." She proudly held up the silver dress.

"Trust me. Marriage isn't what it's cracked up to be."

"It is when you take on a *partner* and not a dependent like Ricky."

Peyton bit back her retort and snatched the outfit. What was the point of arguing? They could easily be at it all night. Once she was in the shower, she mulled over how her sisters placed way too much value on being married.

True, she would love to be in a good, loving relationship, but she wasn't too sure if marriage would fit her lifestyle or her sense of independence. "Better not mention that to anyone," she mumbled and shut off the water.

For the next hour, she and Joey prepared to hit New York's nightlife. However, she held little hope that her evening would be any better than her day. She was tired, hungry, and showing more skin than was probably legal.

"Damn, girl. You look hot." Joey clapped her hands.

"I look like I should be in a rap video," Peyton corrected, but admitted inwardly that she did feel sexy in the skimpy number. "All right. Let's just get this over with," she huffed when Joey came out and performed a pirouette to show off her outfit. "It's nine o'clock. I want to be back in bed by one."

Joey's expression dropped as she looked at her watch. "That's hardly enough time—"

"Take it or leave it. I have an appointment in the morning that I plan to keep." Peyton grabbed her jacket and headed toward the door.

Joey sighed as she followed her.

With a firm hold on his silver cane, Lincoln maneuvered through a throng of fine women and testosterone-charged men to make it to a seat at the bar. "A scotch on the rocks, please," he ordered, and then glanced around to see if he could spot his buddy Tyrone.

As he glanced around he felt more than a tad out of place. Not that he didn't appreciate the surrounding beauties, but damn, did they have to play the music so loud in this place?

"One scotch on the rocks," the Alicia Keys lookalike bartender said, smiling.

"Thanks." Lincoln flashed her his set of dimples and watched as her eyes lit up before she was called to the other end of the bar.

"You still got it." Tyrone's rough laugh filled Lincoln's ears before his heavy hand pounded his back. "Did I lie or is this place off the hook?"

"It's definitely . . . something." Lincoln took a sip

of his drink and glanced at his watch. "Well, don't forget we can't stay long. I have that meeting in the morning."

The deejay changed the record and apparently it was a club favorite, judging by the way the crowd's volume accelerated and how everyone, including the ones at the bar, broke out dancing.

"Hey, don't turn into a fuddy-duddy on me tonight," Tyrone yelled. "This is my first time in this city and I want to see for myself if this is a city that never sleeps."

"You're going to have to find that out on your own." Lincoln drained his drink and signaled to the bartender for a refill. "I heard this P.J. Garner is one of the best agents around, and I'm not going to blow this opportunity."

Tyrone bobbed his head and continued to shout. "I hear you." He turned to the bartender. "I'll have a vodka and tonic."

"You got it." The sexy bartender winked and disappeared.

Tyrone glanced back at Lincoln. "You're not the only one who can rake in the ladies."

"Glad to hear it." He lifted his new drink and turned again to survey the crowd. A flash of silver splayed over a perfectly curved hip caught his eye and caused his heart to skip a beat. He did a double take, but the vision disappeared.

Lincoln lowered his drink on the bar and clutched his cane as he stood up for a better view of the crowd. "Where did she go?"

"Where did who go?"

"That woman," he said, and then held his breath while he carefully scanned the club.

"I see a lot of women. Do you want to be a little more specific?"

"I don't know. She was just . . ." He caught the flash of silver again. "Watch my drink. I'll be back."

He squeezed through the tight crowd again with his chin held high and his gaze locked on those luscious round hips.

When he was finally within inches of her, a tall broad-shouldered brother blocked him and asked his silver-clad goddess to the dance floor. To his disappointment, she accepted and allowed the man to place his large hand against the small of her back and guide her along.

He followed them without thinking. In some ways, he swore that he was having an out-of-body experience and his body was simply subjected to some strange magnetic force. It wasn't until he reached the dance floor that he was able to take in the full package of the woman who had captivated him—and he was in no way disappointed.

Long, curvy pecan-tanned legs were attached to those voluptuous hips, not to mention sexy six-pack abs, and a mind-blowing cleavage that had his mouth salivating. By the time his gaze made it to her heart-shaped face, full lips, and sparkling doe-shaped eyes, his heart was racing as if he'd just completed the New York Marathon.

She was positively breathtaking—and one hell of a dancer. She was partnered with some lucky quarter back-looking dude and was dancing circles around him.

With each gyration of the hip, or delectable bounce of her apple bottom, Lincoln felt the room's temperature jumped a whopping ten degrees. He moved toward them, desperately wanting to cut in on her partner's action.

However, he was again sidetracked when a woman in red just started dancing with him. They were standing right next to his silver temptress, so he played along and started dancing with the woman in red.

Then it happened. The silver beauty glanced up

and met Lincoln's gaze. She smiled, but continued to gyrate against the quarterback.

It was then that he felt the brush of his partner's tush against "Linc Jr." He played it off and continued dancing, despite his cane. What was exotic about the whole thing was that they were dirty-dancing with different partners, and yet their eyes never left each other's.

By the end of the first song, Lincoln was sweating up a storm. Yet, he still didn't cut in on the quarterback. Instead, he watched another brother take her partner's place. In return, Lincoln grabbed another woman, all the while maintaining eye contact with the silver goddess.

Lincoln couldn't remember having so much fun and even wondered if what they were doing was considered foreplay. Lord knows it sure felt like it.

He lost track of how many songs had played and he was just thinking that it was time he made his move when his current partner leaned over, draped one arm around his neck, and directed his chin downward so that their eyes would meet.

"You sure are a good dancer, *papí*," the Spanish beauty complimented. "Are you new in town? You don't look like you're from around here."

"Yeah." He pulled his gaze away to glance beside him and was stunned to find that his silver lady was gone. Lincoln immediately stopped dancing. "Where did she go?"

"C'mon, *papí*. Don't you want to show me a good time?" She slid her other arm around his neck and plastered her body against him.

"Excuse me," he said, pulling at one of her arms. "I have to find someone." He broke away and once again found himself enmeshed in a crowd of dancing people. To his amazement, it was as if his silver lady had just disappeared into thin air.

It was difficult, but he made a loop around the dance floor and came up empty. His mind raced through the possibilities and he made a quick jaunt around crowded tables and then found himself back at the bar.

"Maybe the ladies' room," he mumbled. The pain in his ankle that he'd ignored on the dance floor throbbed mercilessly, but he continued toward the alcove where the restrooms were located.

"Yo, dude. Where are you headed?" Tyrone's voice boomed at him.

Until that moment, Lincoln hadn't fully comprehended what he was doing. He turned to faced his buddy and found him with a scantily clad woman.

"I, uh . . ."

"Please tell me you weren't about to do what I think you were."

"Are you looking for someone?" the lady at Tyrone's side inquired.

Lincoln perked up. "As a matter of fact I was." He straightened. "Would you mind ducking in there and seeing if a . . . um, a woman dressed in a two-piece short silver number—"

"You mean the woman you were staring at on the dance floor?"

Lincoln glanced at Tyrone.

His buddy just shrugged. "We're not the only ones who noticed."

"Yes, that's the girl."

The woman looked to Tyrone. "Well, she just left a few minutes ago, didn't she?"

"I believe so."

Lincoln groaned with disbelief as his heart plunged to the pit of his stomach. "Damn."

Chapter 7

In the middle of 2i's dance floor, Peyton spotted her prey and he couldn't have been a finer specimen of a man. Her gaze skimmed over dark, rich chocolaty skin and a body that rivaled a Greek god's. However, it was the stranger's eyes and dimpled cheeks that nearly melted her lacy Cosabella thong.

She pushed him into a chair and began an impromptu lap dance. From beneath his intense gaze, she felt like a member of the Pussycat dancers and her performance was an erotic foray for his eyes only. In the back of her mind, she realized that didn't make much sense, seeing as how they were in the middle of a crowded dance club. And yet, it made perfect sense.

The crowd surrounded them and joined the act. Their cheers encouraged her, but her attention never left Mr. Tall, Dark, and Handsome. She straddled him in a provocative lap dance that escalated her body's temperature and quickened her heartbeat. Moving against him, she felt his hard body beneath his black linen suit and she could tell by her bottom's constant grind against his crotch that he was working with quite an impressive package.

This was more than just dancing, it was a mating call.

Peyton roamed her hands along his chest and, on a naughty impulse, she ripped open his shirt and exposed his bare, tight muscled chest. . . .

A loud ringing jarred Peyton from her deep slumber. She jerked up in bed and glanced guiltily around. For a moment, she didn't recognize her surroundings.

The phone rang again.

"Are you going to answer that?" Joey groaned from the other bed.

Peyton frowned and then picked up the phone. "Hello."

"Ms. Garner. This is your six-thirty wake-up call."

"Thanks," she mumbled and hung up. She sat there for a while as bits and pieces of her dream flashed inside her head. A smile fluttered across her lips as an image of a pair of intense black eyes twinkled back at her. Who was that guy and how come they don't make them like that in California?

Peyton swung her legs over the edge of the bed and then glanced over at her snoozing sister. "Great. She gets to sleep and I have to go to work."

Climbing out of bed, Peyton first went to her sister's suitcase to see if she could find something decent to wear to her eight o'clock meeting. She was worried for a moment when she pulled out one hoochie-mama outfit after another. At long last, she found one pair of slacks and a reasonable blouse.

She took a record-breaking shower and then hurried to apply her makeup.

"I still can't get over you and that dude on the

floor last night," Joey said, yawning from the bathroom's doorway. "I've never seen you like that."

Peyton frowned. "What do you mean?"

"What do I mean? Hell, I thought everyone at the club should be paying you for that performance."

"I was just dancing." Peyton concentrated on tweezing her eyebrows.

"My ass." Joey laughed. "Why didn't you just jump the guy and get it over with?"

"Okay, now you're being ridiculous."

"Uh-huh." She settled her hands on her hips. "If you want my opinion, I think you got a little freak in you."

Try as she might, Peyton couldn't help but laugh.

"I have to hand it to you though. Brother man was fine."

Peyton met Joey's gaze in the mirror. "He was, wasn't he?"

"Did you ever get the digits?"

Peyton went back to her eyebrows. "No, I didn't."

Joey's eyes widened. "You have to be kidding me. Why not? It was obvious the guy was into you."

"Haven't you ever heard the edict, 'what happens at the club stays at the club'?"

Joey rolled her eyes.

"C'mon. That's why people give out fake names and numbers when they go to those places. You just go for a good time. Club romances are doomed from the start. Everyone goes there puttin' on a front. It takes entirely too much work to try and plow through the layers of horse manure to find out who you're really dating."

Joey stared at her through the mirror. "Has anyone ever told you that you're high maintenance?"

Peyton rummaged through her makeup bag. "Whatever."

"No. You are. You have a whole list of complaints

for nearly every type of man or every meeting situation. It's like you can't find the good in anything."

"That's not true. Well . . . not anymore. I know what kind of man I want."

"Oh yeah, Mr. Handyman. How could I forget?" Joey rolled her eyes and moved farther into the bathroom so that she stood just inches behind her sister. "New York is crawling with construction workers. Why don't you just hang out around those sites to see what you can bag?"

"You don't get it," Peyton huffed and grabbed a brush. "I don't want a beer-guzzling, ass-scratching, and 'baby, where's the remote control?' type of man. I want a nice combination of—"

"High maintenance."

"Am not!" Peyton turned away from the mirror and stormed back into their room. "I'm borrowing an outfit. Maybe later this afternoon we can hit a few stores so I'll have something to wear."

"Cool." Joey jumped back into her bed. "I'm going to get a few more hours of shut-eye while you're gone."

"You do that." Peyton finished getting dressed and grabbed her purse. But as she left the room, she mumbled under her breath, "I'm *not* high maintenance."

Lincoln woke up with a hard-on.

All night he had dreamed of his silver goddess and cursed himself for the lost opportunity. Why had he waited so long to approach her? It didn't make sense and it wasn't like him.

You have to get up or you're going to be late. Lincoln moaned and wanted nothing more than to return to his dream where a hot apple-bottom woman ruled his world. However, the moment he closed his eyes the phone rang next to his head.

Groaning, he shot out an arm and picked up the receiver. "Hello."

"Good morning, Mr. Carver. This is your seven-thirty wake-up call."

"Yeah, thanks." He clunked the receiver back onto the phone and sat up. He gave himself exactly two minutes to shake all thoughts of curvy limbs and luscious lips out of his head. It was time to focus on business.

Hobbling into the bathroom, he quickly jumped into the shower—a cold one—and thought back to what a wild ride the past three months had been. Thanks to the metal rod in his ankle, his firefighting career had come to a screeching halt—sort of. He was approached by the city to take a desk job as a fire inspector, which he might accept if there was no future in his being an iron sculptor.

He couldn't help but laugh at himself. He picked one hell of a time in his life to pursue being an artist. He had to face it, he was no spring chicken. Forty loomed around the corner.

He finished his frolic in the shower and performed a quick shave and brushed his teeth. Everything took him a record-breaking fifteen minutes to complete and then he was out the door with his portfolio.

In no time Lincoln was rushing past Rockefeller Center and over to the New York Palace Hotel. It wasn't until he breezed into the breathtaking lobby that he experienced a wave of nervous anxiety. What if he wasn't any good? What if this agent hated his work?

He stepped into the elevator along with a multitude of ritzy, stylish men and women that quickly made him feel like a fish out of water in his casual khakis and crisp, clean white shirt. With great difficulty, he pushed all doubt out of his mind and concentrated on all the positive feedback he'd received in Atlanta for his work.

"Raw," "innovative," and even "genius" had been the words of praise he'd received. It took a lot for him to show people what had long been considered a hobby—*people* being his best friend, Tyrone, and the three stooges. Then again, they weren't exactly the types who appreciated art. Art, of course, being outside of pinup posters of Tracy Bingham.

The elevator stopped on the thirty-ninth floor. He stepped off and entered the Executive Lounge. It was a rare event for him to be nervous, but he gave himself a mental pep talk and was ready to take the plunge.

"Can I help you, sir?" a bright and bubbly blonde asked, staring up at him.

"Yes, I have a business appointment with a P.J. Garner."

"Yes, sir. She's waiting for you. Please follow me."

Lincoln fell in line behind the hostess and found himself still fighting his anxiety.

The hostess pushed open a door to a private meeting room. "Ms. Garner, your appointment has arrived," she said, and then stepped back to allow Lincoln access.

Lincoln crossed the threshold, lifted his gaze, and froze when he met the eyes of his silver goddess. "Well, I'll be damned."

Chapter 8

Peyton couldn't speak.

How could she? Surely, there were no words suitable for an awkward moment like this. Out of desperation, she closed her eyes and prayed the handsome image would change by the time she reopened them.

It didn't.

"Lincoln Carver?" she asked, in an uncharacteristic squeaky voice.

He nodded and his smile widened. "P.J. Garner?"

"I don't believe this." Her entire body felt hot with embarrassment as she cleared her throat and offered her hand. "Nice to meet you—finally." His large hand swallowed hers, and despite the feel of calluses they were amazingly gentle.

"Likewise."

What a voice, she marveled. It sort of reminded her of someone, but she couldn't remember who. When he smiled, her gaze immediately lowered to his deep dimpled cheeks. *Now, this is a man.*

Peyton pulled her hand away and gestured to a vacant chair. "If you're ready, we can get started."

He lifted a single brow and then headed over to the chair. "You know I was disappointed when you disappeared last night."

While his back was to her, she exhaled and turned to close the door. "I was just . . . I wasn't quite myself." She returned to her own chair, forcing a plastic smile. It was definitely going to be a challenge to get this meeting onto the right track, especially since she felt that her credibility had been shot.

"Okay," Peyton said. "Let's just forget about last night and focus on the matter at hand."

"I'd rather not."

His rich voice melted like hot chocolate over her while his gaze performed a slow drag over her face. Her heart muscles tightened and made it difficult to breathe.

"Would you like some coffee?" She stood again. "I just had some delivered a few minutes ago."

"Sure. I could go for a cup. I didn't get too much sleep last night."

"You're not the only one," Peyton mumbled as she turned toward the coffeemaker.

"I'm sorry. What did you say?"

"Oh, nothing," she lied, and then rolled her eyes. This man was the hottest thing walking and, God help her, she couldn't stop thinking about her erotic dream.

"How would you like your coffee?"

"Black," he answered.

Surprised, she glanced over her shoulder, but found him staring at her bottom. *Typical.*

"Cornel Dyson is a good friend of mine. I was surprised by his referral. Usually, he's very protective of newly discovered talent. How did you two meet?" she asked, pouring his coffee.

Carver laughed. "My best friend pulled him over

for a traffic violation and then recognized his name from some feature in *Creative Loafing*."

"Are you kidding me?"

"No. It's a pretty popular paper. They cover a lot of art stuff in Atlanta."

She returned to the table and handed him his cup. "You're telling me that Cornel referred you to me because he—"

"He was trying to get out of a speeding ticket. Thanks."

Peyton was going to kill Dyson. He never met with Carver, he just pawned him off on her. After taking a deep breath, she was determined to remain professional. "So, you say you're from Atlanta?"

"Actually, I live in Marietta. It's a suburb of the city."

Peyton settled back into her chair, feeling grateful that she had successfully maneuvered away from last night's shenanigans to a safer topic. "I have a brother in Decatur. Are you far from there?"

"Actually, I used to work out in Decatur. It's about thirty-five, forty miles from me."

"Yikes, that's a distance."

"It's not too bad. Everyone is pretty much used to traveling in that area."

"I doubt you know him. He's pretty new there. Anyway, let's get started. What did you bring for me, Mr. Carver?"

"Please, call me Lincoln." His onyx gaze held hers prisoner as he reached for his portfolio. "It's what my friends call me."

Breathe. Just remember to breathe. "All right then, Lincoln. Let's see what you got."

He placed his portfolio onto the table and slid it over to her. "I hope that you like what you see," he said.

She lowered her gaze to the first black-and-white

photo. *Hell, I did that the minute you walked through the door.*

"Why the smile?" he asked.

"Hmm?" She glanced up and forced her best innocent look.

"You were smiling." Amusement sparkled in his eyes and hugged his lips.

Damn, he's sexy. "Nothing. I like this." She returned her attention to the photographs. The images of the iron sculptures were quite good. Actually, they were outstanding.

"How long have you been doing this?" she inquired.

Lincoln braided his fingers and looked along with her as she turned the pages. "Twelve or thirteen years. It's pretty much been a hobby."

Peyton leaned in to study the photographs and couldn't help but be impressed. She was also beginning to feel a familiar bubble of excitement. In her mind she was already running through a list of dealers and museums that would be interested in some of the pieces.

"What are you wearing?" he asked suddenly.

"Huh?" She glanced over at him. Her heart leaped at his closeness.

"Your perfume. I'm trying to place it. It's soft, clean—"

"It's soap."

He blinked. "Well, it . . . uh, suits you."

"Thank you," she said, struggling to keep a straight face. Her gaze traveled back to his work. "How many shows have you done?" she asked.

"Shows?" Lincoln threw his head back and laughed.

The rich vibrato of his laughter instantly had her twitching in her seat. How in the world was this man doing all these things to her when he hadn't so much as laid a finger on her?

"I've never done a show," he said. "But does this mean you think they're good?"

She reached for her coffee and took a sip while she weighed her words. "Art is a funny business," she began. "One of the most frustrating things is that it's also very subjective."

"One man's trash is another man's treasure?"

"Something like that." She smiled.

As their gazes locked again, Lincoln folded his arms and leaned back in his chair. "What do *you* see—trash or treasure?"

She immediately sensed that he wasn't talking about his work. Their eyes met again and her body's wires threatened to short-circuit. And yet, she managed to remain calm. "I see a man with a lot of potential."

Lincoln nodded. "Do you *see* yourself accepting my invitation to dinner?"

"Dinner?" She shifted in her chair and fought like hell to prevent the corners of her lips from curling into a smile.

"We both have to eat," he said. "And with this being my first time in New York, I don't know my way around town. Maybe you can help me in that department?"

"You found 2i's pretty good."

"I'd be willing to go back if you'd go with me." He shrugged. "Maybe we can finally get that dance together."

Despite the temptation, Peyton laughed and shook her head. "We're supposed to be talking about business."

"We can talk about business tonight. You can tell me then if you've decided to represent me."

Her eyes fell back to the photographs. They were good. "Truth is, I already have plans for tonight."

"Break them."

She laughed. "I can't break them."

Lincoln leaned forward on his arms. "And why not? I can tell you *want* to have dinner with me."

She continued to be amused by him. "You're pretty sure of yourself."

"Don't tell me you're turned off by a confident man?"

"Confident or arrogant?" she challenged.

"Are you sure you're qualified to tell the difference?"

"Qualified?" She blinked and forced out a laugh, cringing at just how hollow it sounded.

Lincoln's smile widened. "How about a test?"

Peyton's brows lifted.

"A small test. If you pass, then you're off the hook and you don't have to have dinner with me tonight."

"I don't have to do that anyway."

"But if you fail," he went on as if he hadn't heard her, "it's Citarella's. You and me."

"I thought you didn't know anything about New York?"

"I read about it somewhere." He winked. "So what do you say?"

"About what—taking a test? I don't want to take your silly test."

"Forfeit counts as a failure."

She rolled her eyes. "There you go being arrogant again. Has it occurred to you that I simply don't *want* to go out with you? Not all women go for the . . . muscular, tall, dark—"

"And handsome type?" He smiled. "Yeah, I heard there was an underground movement of women seeking out short, morbidly obese, ugly men."

"You're not funny," she said with a deadpan expression.

"So charming is off your list, too?"

"I didn't say that."

Lincoln shrugged and held up his hands in surrender. "I think you're right. We shouldn't go out. I can already tell you're a bit on the high-maintenance side." He flipped another page of the portfolio. "So back to my work."

"I am not high maintenance," she retorted.

Lincoln looked up while another shrug tugged his shoulders. "If you say so." He returned his attention back to the pictures. "Now, this is one of my earlier works—"

"I wouldn't have any problems dating a . . . heavy-set guy," she huffed. "And there's nothing wrong with dating someone who isn't *GQ* material either. In fact, I find pretty boys to be . . ."

". . . Arrogant," he filled in for her.

"Exactly!"

His eyes narrowed. "You know what my problem is with your type?"

"My type?"

"Too judgmental."

"Judgmental?"

"Do you always repeat everything someone says? You're starting to sound like a parrot."

"A parr—" She clamped her mouth shut.

Lincoln leaned back in his chair and smiled. "I bet you try to put everyone in a box. 'He's attractive, so I can't go out with him. He's too confident, so I can't go out with him.'" He shook his head. "High maintenance."

"Mr. Carver, I don't think I'll be able to represent you."

"I agree," he said, seemingly unruffled by her announcement. "You don't strike me as the type who's capable of separating business and pleasure."

"That's not true."

"Yeah, right."

Rattled by his obvious disbelief, she ranted on, "I assure you, Mr. Carver, I'm a complete professional."

"So," he began, rolling his eyes toward the ceiling as if considering a hypothetical scenario. "If we were in a passionate, intimate, personal affair . . ."

"It would never infringe or disrupt our business relationship."

His onyx gaze centered on her. "Prove it. Have dinner with me tonight."

She laughed. "Nice try." She crossed her arms and studied him. "You're a tricky little devil, aren't you?"

He shrugged with an easy smile. "I thought a little reverse psychology would help my case. I'm interested, and everything in my body tells me that you are too."

She started to deny it, but stopped. She was attracted to him—*very* attracted. "One date?"

"Just one," he said.

Peyton drew a deep breath and considered him. He was different, there was no doubt about that. And he was definitely a man who knew how to take charge. She liked that, but it was his arrogance that disturbed her the most. "All right, Mr. Carver. You're on." What was she saying? The man had called her a parrot. "Meet me tonight in the lobby at eight o'clock." She slowly stood up and closed the portfolio.

"It's a date." He smiled.

Peyton turned and walked toward the door. "Do try not to be late." She tossed him a smile over her shoulder and slipped out the door.

Once she was in the hallway, her smile disappeared as she blazed a trail toward the elevator. "I must be out of my mind."

She pressed the down button on the elevator and waited. "He's just going to be like all the others."

"I'm sensing that your heart isn't in this."

Peyton jumped and swiveled toward the velvety baritone. "You shouldn't sneak up on people like that!"

"My apologies." Lincoln frowned. "You know we don't have to go out."

The elevator arrived.

"So what do I get if you forfeit?"

They stepped into the small compartment.

Lincoln shrugged. "Fine. We'll go out, but do try to sound more excited about it. You're starting to give me a complex."

Peyton punched for the thirtieth floor. "We wouldn't want that."

"I have a feeling this is going to be an interesting date," he said calmly.

"I was just thinking the same thing."

He laughed. "Do you always have to have the last word?"

She chuckled along with him. "Do you?"

"Oh boy."

"You know what I hate about *your* type?" she challenged, with a painted-on smile. "You can't appreciate a woman with a good head on her shoulders. You think everyone wants you just because you're good looking. Well, I'm not impressed. I prefer a man with a little more substance than—"

Lincoln kissed her.

And it was no ordinary kiss, none like she'd ever experienced, anyway. His lips were soft, but his mouth was hard—hungry. His tongue delved into her mouth and destroyed her every wall of defense with smooth skillful strokes.

The portfolio dropped to the floor, freeing her arms so they could glide gently around his broad shoulders.

Was that her moaning? *Please, say I have a little more dignity than that.* She didn't.

She felt small and yet protected in his embrace. Before now, only her father had ever made her feel protected. How strange for her to think of that now. Just when her mind had acclimated to staying cocooned against him, the elevator stopped and the doors slid open.

Lincoln lifted his head and ended the kiss. "I believe this is your floor."

"What?" she questioned through a clouded haze.

"Your floor."

His arms slid away and she missed them immediately. "Huh? Yeah." She stepped back and nearly fell when her legs failed to support her.

"Whoa." His arms returned to prevent her from taking a nasty spill. "Are you all right?"

"Fine," she whispered and ran a hand through her hair. "I'm just fine."

The doors started to close and Lincoln released her to block them.

Peyton used the time to grab the portfolio off the floor and compose herself. "Well," she said, unable to meet his eyes. "I guess I'll see you tonight then?"

"Eight o'clock," he confirmed.

She nodded while her lips trembled through an awkward smile. "See you tonight." She stepped out of the small compartment with her head held too high.

"Ms. Garner?"

"Yes?"

A wide smile broke beneath his twinkling gaze as

he stepped back into the compartment. "You're a great kisser."

The doors slid closed.

Peyton slumped back against the wall and whispered, "You're not so bad your damn self."

Chapter 9

Lincoln twirled his silver cane as he strolled down the crowded sidewalks of Manhattan. Like last night, he was able to suppress all feelings of pain in his leg, while his thoughts focused on Ms. Garner. *What man wouldn't like that kind of spice in his life?* he mused.

By the time he returned to his hotel, he was floating on cloud nine and singing R. Kelly's "Your Body's Callin' Aloud."

"Hey, man." Tyrone's voice boomed behind him. "You're back already?"

Lincoln flashed his friend, who was dressed head to toe in New York Yankees memorabilia, a smile as they both stopped in the elevator bay.

"So, how did it go?" Tyrone asked.

"Better than I could *ever* have expected."

"That good, huh? Does that mean we're about to be big ballers now?"

"We?" Lincoln laughed. "What is this 'we' crap?"

The men stepped into an empty elevator.

"Oh, it's like that now?" Tyrone said, bobbing his head. "You're not going to hook a brother up for discovering you?"

Lincoln pressed the button for their floor. "Get a hold of yourself. I went to meet an agent, not a buyer. Hell, there's no guarantee that I'll ever make any money at this."

"You better if you're thinking about leaving the fire department. You're too old to be a starving artist."

"I have a little saved up."

Tyrone shook his head. "And when that's all gone?"

"I'll manage," Lincoln said, but he was beginning to feel uncomfortable. Did he have enough saved up? Would he ever sell anything? "I thought you came to be my moral support?"

"I did. I am."

"Then how come I feel like I'm about to have a heart attack? I was fine until you started grilling me." He pressed his palm against his forehead. "I have about sixty thousand in the bank and—"

"Sixty? Hot damn. What bank did you knock over?"

Arriving at their floor, they stepped out of the elevator.

"It's called being frugal, my friend," Lincoln said. "Live beneath one's means, as my father likes to preach."

Tyrone rolled his eyes. "Like father like son."

"Please don't say that." Lincoln slid his key card in the door and then entered the room. "I'm nothing like my father."

"If you say so." Tyrone laughed. "I don't know what's the big deal. Your dad's a pretty cool guy."

Lincoln sighed at the back and forth of the conversation. "Can we please just focus? You'll never guess who P.J. Garner is." He slowly lowered himself into a chair. The throb in his ankle had finally gotten his attention.

"It's someone you know?" Tyrone asked incredulously.

"Not yet, but after tonight I will."

* * *

"What are you so upset about?" Joey asked, watching Peyton storm around the room. "Did your meeting not go well?"

"I'm not upset." Peyton grabbed her carry-on bag and dug out a copy of the program for the night's art show. "Great, it starts at eight o'clock. I'm going to be late." She dropped onto the bed and tried to think of how she was going to manage to show up late for Yosa's first show and also leave early. "What was I thinking, agreeing to go out with him tonight?" she mumbled.

Joey sat next to her. "Go out with who?"

"I *wasn't* thinking," Peyton whispered, and reviewed what had happened between her and Lincoln—all the way up to their departing kiss.

"P.J., are you blushing?"

Peyton's thoughts returned to the present and her gaze slid over to her sister. "What?"

"What am I, talking to myself?" Joey stood, shaking her head. "Keep your little secrets. I *do* have a life, you know."

Peyton heard her, but she didn't comprehend a single word. Her brain was too busy reworking the "Lincoln incident."

Peyton jumped to her feet. "Why did I agree to this? I must be out of my mind."

"I'm feeling a little crazy myself." Joey turned for the door. "I'm out of here. I'll come back when you're finished talking to yourself."

"You know what I hate about men?" Peyton ranted, ignoring whatever her sister was talking about.

"No, I don't care to hear what you hate about men—this time. I'm sure I've heard it before. If not, I'm sure I'll hear about it tomorrow." Joey huffed and settled her hands on her hips. "If men are such a thorn in your side, then maybe you should consider changing up."

"Ha, ha, ha."

"Can we go shopping now—or am I supposed to stay cooped up in this room all weekend?"

Peyton drew a deep breath, counted to ten, and then grabbed her purse. "Shopping it is."

Joey perked up. "Great. We better make sure we pick out something *hot* for your date with whoever he is."

"Let's not make it too hot. I don't want to get into something I can't get out of."

"You mean that hot chick from the club last night?" Tyrone thundered. "She's going to be your new agent?"

"I don't know yet." Lincoln leaned forward and rubbed his ankle. "I had no business on that dance floor last night."

"It looked to me like you knew what you were doing."

"Well, it's killing me now," he said, hating having to complain. "I better take it easy if I don't want to end up back in the hospital."

"Where are your pain pills?" Tyrone stood. "Maybe you should take a few of them."

"Nah, those things always knock me flat on my butt and I have a date."

"Since when? Wait. Don't tell me you're going out with the agent."

Lincoln looked up and winked at his buddy. "All right, I won't tell you."

"You sly dog. Is it business or pleasure?"

"The jury is still out," he joked, and thought back to his meeting that morning. "But if it comes down to a choice, I'd rather have the latter."

"You think your luck with women has changed?" Tyrone asked.

Moaning, Lincoln eased down in his chair. "That's a tough call, but this P.J.—I wonder what that stands for."

"Now look who has trouble focusing."

"Like I was saying, Ms. Garner is going to be a handful. I can already tell that she's some type of control freak, not to mention high maintenance."

"In that case, I only have one piece of advice for you, my friend: *run.*"

"There's a fire in her eyes though—a challenge. She's been burned before, I'm willing to bet my life on it."

"There's a word that describes women like that: *bitter.*"

Lincoln shook his head. "Nah, she's harmless. Probably just needs to be taken down a peg or two."

"Now, that's just being arrogant," Tyrone said, standing up. "I'm heading out. I want to take one of those tour buses up to Harlem. You want to join me?"

"No, I'm going to call room service and rest my leg for a while. Maybe we can go out this afternoon before my date?"

"You got it," Tyrone agreed, and then left the room.

Lincoln waited until the door clicked closed before he reached over and snatched up the phone. In his excitement, he fumbled the number a few times before he was able to get Flex on his cell phone.

"Hello."

"You are brilliant," Lincoln raved.

"Well . . . I don't like to brag." Flex chuckled. "Where are you and what was I so brilliant about?"

"Tyrone and I are up in New York. I came up to meet this art agent—"

"All right, man. You decided to go for it. Good for

you. You know Peyton is a . . . uh, well, she knows a lot of people in the art world. Maybe when you do a portfolio I can ask her about some referrals."

"I might have to take you up on that because the agent I met today, I'm more interested in a personal relationship than a professional."

"Plunging back into the dating arena?"

"What can I say? Women may be a complication, but they are also my weakness. And that stuff you said about Type-A women personalities was dead on the money." Lincoln laughed. "You really do know about the woman's psyche."

"Five sisters will do that."

"You're officially my relationship guru. I had this woman so turned around she didn't know what hit her. It's all thanks to you, man."

"It went that well?"

"We're going out tonight. I have to tell you, this one is a real ball buster, too. She has a chip so big on her shoulder it'll probably take a bulldozer to knock it off."

The line vibrated with Flex's laughter. "Sounds like you really know how to pick them."

Lincoln's thoughts drifted to the carefree and uninhibited dancer from last night to the business professional he'd met this morning. "This one is different."

"They all are."

"I'm not going to be able to win her without your help."

"I am at your service."

Peyton couldn't remember ever being so nervous about a date. It was also the first time she felt like she had a point to prove. She wasn't high maintenance or judgmental. Men were the ones with preconceived notions of the opposite sex. They didn't know how to handle a woman with more than half a brain or one who was comfortable with her own sexuality.

"How much longer are you going to be in the bathroom?" Joey shouted through the door.

"Just a few more minutes." Peyton glanced at herself in the mirror and hated how her shoulder-length locks weren't cooperating. She tossed down the curling iron and cursed under her breath.

On cue, the bathroom door swung open.

"Are you all right? What's going on in here?" Joey's gaze swept over her sister. "Are you going out like that?"

Peyton drew a deep breath and counted to ten. However, even that didn't help eliminate her anxiety. "I'm just under a lot of stress," she offered as an excuse.

Joey smirked and folded her arms. "I never would've believed it if I hadn't seen it with my own eyes. This guy has gotten under your skin."

"Don't be ridiculous." Peyton grabbed a brush and attacked her hair. "This guy is just an arrogant jerk."

"Whom you happen to be going out with." Joey cringed, watching her sister, and then snatched the brush out of her hand. "You're making my head hurt. Sit down."

Peyton opened her mouth to protest, but one look at Joey's "take no lip" expression and she popped a squat on top of the toilet bowl and allowed her sister to take over.

"So tell me what you're so worried about."

"Who said I was worried?"

Joey yanked Peyton's hair.

"Ouch."

"Oops. The brush must have slipped. What were you saying?"

Peyton reached to rub her sore scalp, but received a whack on the hand. "Ouch. What's with you?"

"Nothing. I just hate it when you lie to me." Joey forced her chin up so their eyes would meet. "I'm older and know when you're lying."

Peyton wanted to protest again, but thought it wouldn't exactly be a great idea to show up bald for her date.

"I'm still waiting for an answer," Joey added. "You're not getting out of here until you fess up."

Drawing a deep breath, Peyton once again tried to relax. She hated this—telephone, telegraph, tell-a-Joey. Peyton felt a tug on her hair and understood the warning. "I'm just worried . . . I won't make a good . . . impression on this guy."

When Joey remained quiet, Peyton continued, "He's . . . different. I initially thought I had him pegged and then in the next moment I found myself . . . challenged by him."

"That's a good thing, right?"

Peyton shrugged. "I'm not sure. I'm, sort of, used to being in control."

"How do you explain that brain fart you had with Ricky?"

"Ricky was harmless," she said, waving off the question. "According to my therapist, I married him for the sake of being married. Yes, he was a bum, but he was a controllable bum."

"Since when did you start seeing a therapist?"

Peyton hesitated. It was too late to turn back now. "Since Mom passed away."

Joey's hands stilled. "I had no idea."

"It's not a big deal."

Joey took the curling iron to Peyton's hair. "So, you have control issues—and this recent fixation on finding a 'manly man' is because you're finally looking for someone to take control?"

Peyton frowned "I didn't say all of that."

"You didn't have to. You're not the only one with a therapist."

The sisters' gazes met for a brief moment before they burst out laughing.

All this time, Peyton thought her sisters left no stone unturned when it came to snooping into each other's lives, and now it was actually refreshing to learn that she wasn't the only one who kept a few secrets.

"C'mon, take a look." Joey pulled her up and turned her to face the mirror.

A wide smile covered Peyton's face. "I'm going to knock his socks off."

Chapter 10

Lincoln succumbed to the pain and popped two painkillers seconds before he headed out for his date. Within minutes, the merciless throb in his ankle subsided and he was able to review all the information Flex had downloaded into his brain.

"Men are from Mars and women are from Venus."

In the past, Lincoln never had trouble meeting or dating women. Invariably, the differences between the sexes were what cost him the relationship.

Really, what was wrong with watching a lot of football or wanting to have a night out with the guys? Did a relationship mean that you had to spend every waking moment with the woman? And what was with them calling so much during the day? If you weren't with them, then you had to be on the phone with them.

The Palace Hotel came into view and Lincoln couldn't believe how badly his stomach twisted into knots. That couldn't be a good sign, *could it?* He glanced at his watch. He was ten minutes early.

Once he was in the lobby of the grand hotel, he again felt out of place. The life of a public servant didn't normally afford him the opportunity to stroll such opulent halls. Hell, the only way he would even be in a place like this was if the building was on fire.

He took a seat in a beautiful ornate chair that was apparently purchased more for decoration than comfort, but regardless, he dozed off.

"Mr. Carver?"

Lincoln woke with a jolt. "Huh, what?"

"Are you all right?" P.J. asked, frowning.

Lincoln cleared his throat and smiled at the beauty dressed in a sapphire shoulderless number that hugged her every curve. This was the classy P.J. Garner—another dimension of her diamond personality. Just as he remembered from the club, she had curves in all the right places. "I'm better now that an angel has arrived."

Her eyebrows rose at the honey-coated praise. "Poetry isn't your strong suit."

"Everyone's a critic." He pushed himself up with his cane. "My point is that you look ravishing."

"Thank you," she said, as her gaze skittered away. "You clean up well yourself."

Lincoln glanced down at his one and only black suit. "Oh, this old thing?" He offered her his arm. "It's just something that I threw together."

P.J. smiled and looped her arm through his. "I hope you don't mind, but I absolutely have to make an appearance at the Museum of African Art. One of my artists has a show tonight."

"By all means," he said, escorting her out of the door. "I made our reservations at the Citarella for nine-thirty. Will that be enough time?"

"That should be perfect," she said, smiling.

The doorman hailed a taxi and within minutes they were off. The silence inside the cab, Lincoln noted, was strained and more than uncomfortable. Flex said that women loved good listeners, but wouldn't the woman have to talk in order for him to listen?

"About this morning," he began with no clue as to how to end.

"Yes?" She glanced at him.

"I probably shouldn't have kissed you like that," he settled on saying.

"Oh," she said, and played with her hands on her lap.

"I'm not saying I'm sorry," he added. "I just hope I didn't scare you."

"Oh no. You didn't," she assured him, and straightened in her seat. "I rather . . . kind of enjoyed it."

It was all he needed to hear before a smile curved his lips and his arms slid behind her head on the seat. "So tell me about yourself, Ms. Garner. Why are you such a mixed bag of contradictions?"

"I'm not sure I understand you."

As he met her twinkling gaze, Lincoln felt a tightening in his chest. His eyes lowered to her full lips and he experienced another overwhelming urge to kiss her.

"I'm talking about the different signals. One minute I feel you're really into me, and then in the next it seems like you can't stand me."

Her gaze lowered.

"So which is it?" he asked. "Do you really want to be with me tonight or are you still trying to prove a point?" He forced himself to wait through the long silence, and just when he thought he had his answer she responded.

"Yes." She looked at him again. "I want to be here with you tonight."

He smiled. "Glad to hear it."

"Here we are," the cabdriver announced.

Lincoln reached for his wallet. "Keep the change." He handed over a few bills, climbed out of the cab, and rushed to the other side to open the door for his date. All the while, he wore a grin on his face the size of Texas.

"Thank you," she said, as she accepted his hand and eased out of the cab.

Lincoln thought she looked like a celebrity ready for the red carpet and smelled like a field of fresh flowers. This time he didn't dare ask about the name of her perfume, just in case it ended up being another brand of soap.

They walked arm in arm into the museum, and once inside he wasn't ready to relinquish his hold on her. However, no sooner had they waltzed through the doors than the night's showcased artist, Yosa, whisked her from his side.

"I'll be right back," she mouthed over her shoulder.

Lincoln nodded his understanding and was left to peruse the museum solo.

"Champagne?"

He turned to see a tray thrust in front of him. He reached for a flute and dug into his pockets.

"There's no charge, sir," a pretty waitress informed him with a bright smile. "All drinks are complimentary."

"Ah" was all he could manage to say. Though he hung on to his smile, he suppressed his fish-out-of-water feelings and enjoyed the display of eclectic paintings.

He lost all sense of time as he walked, talked, and sipped his champagne. Somewhere around the middle of the exhibit, a woman joined him and started asking his opinion about the collection.

"By the way, my name is Valeri," she said, extending her hand.

"Lincoln."

"Nice to meet you." She smiled. "I just hate showing up to these things alone."

"I hope I'm not interrupting," a voice came from behind them.

Lincoln and Valeri turned.

P.J. glided next to Lincoln and he looped an arm around her. "Welcome back." He grinned.

"I'm sorry. My mistake," Valeri mumbled, and then disappeared into the crowd.

"Looks like I can't leave you alone for a minute."

He wiggled his brows. "Does that mean you're now mine for the rest of night?"

"I'm afraid so." When P.J. laughed, he realized it was the first time he'd heard those soft lyrical notes. It was as infectious as it was memorable.

"We'd better head out of here if we want to keep our reservations," she whispered close to his ear.

"Let's go." Lincoln turned and set his second flute of champagne on a passing tray. Stifling a yawn, Lincoln suddenly worried about his decision to mix alcohol with his pain medication. When they slipped out of the door, he yawned, and then again as he held open a cab door for her.

Peyton sighed as she waited for Lincoln to join her inside the taxi. So far the night was going better than she had anticipated.

"Citarella," Lincoln informed the driver and then turned his attention to Peyton. "Have you ever been to this place?"

"As a matter of fact, I haven't."

"Good. I want you to associate only *new* experiences with me."

She grinned and was charmed by the corny line. "So when do we get to talk about you?" she asked. "I know you're an artist—one with a lot of potential. But that's all I know."

He hid a yawn behind his hand and then apologized.

Peyton's heart dropped. *Am I boring him?*

"There's not much to tell. As you know, I'm from Georgia. I'm a third-generation firefighter . . . well, used to be, anyway, until I injured my ankle."

Peyton's eyes widened with excitement. "My father and brother are firefighters!"

Lincoln perked up. "You're kidding me."

"Here we are," the cabdriver announced.

As she watched Lincoln pay the driver, suddenly this whole attraction made perfect sense. The protectiveness and security she'd experienced in the elevator weren't just her imagination. Forget Mr. Handyman, she should've been looking for a firefighter all along.

They were late for their reservation, but were still seated rather quickly. However, no sooner had they sat down than she caught him in another yawn. Her ego was going down the tubes.

"Are you sure you're up for dinner? You look more like you need a nap."

After another yawn, he wiped tears from his eyes and tried to explain. "I'm sorry. It's not you. I took pain medication for my ankle this evening. The side effects"—he yawned—"make me extremely drowsy."

She nodded, but the dent wasn't so easily removed from her pride. "Are you sure you don't want to go?"

"Yes. Of course." He reached across the table and squeezed her hand. "I'm having a nice time."

She studied him and smiled when she read sincerity in his gaze. "Me too."

"You're sure you're not finding me too . . . arrogant?" He wiggled his brows.

She laughed. "All right. I might have deserved that. And maybe I was wrong for trying to put you in a box, but you can't tell me you don't do the same thing."

Lincoln opened his mouth, but sensed a trap and closed it.

"Aha! I knew it."

"Wait a minute." He chuckled, holding up his hands. "I didn't say anything."

"Uh-huh. What was all that stuff about women my type?" She enjoyed watching his face flush burgundy. "What's the matter—cat got your tongue?"

"More like trying to proceed with caution. I'm starting to feel like I'm standing in the middle of a minefield."

"Hmm. Smart man."

An older gentleman with a glowing smile greeted them. "Good evening. Welcome to Citarella. My name is Blake and I will be your server this evening. Will this be your first time dining with us?" he asked, handing over the menus.

"Actually it is," Peyton answered and glanced over at Lincoln. She nearly laughed out loud at how his eyes bulged. *He noticed the prices.* She leaned forward and whispered, "Is everything okay?"

He blinked several times before he looked up at her. "Yes, fine. Everything is perfect."

"Great." Peyton returned her attention to their waiter. "Could you give us a few minutes?"

"Certainly. Can I at least take your drink order?"

"A white wine will be fine—you choose."

"Water," Lincoln said, closing his menu. "The medication," he reminded Peyton.

She nodded and waited until they were alone again. "You know, if you'd like to go somewhere else—"

"No, no. This is fine," he assured her with a smile. "Of course, I don't know what half of this stuff is, but I'm open for an adventure if you are." He winked.

His dimpled cheeks melted her armor and she smiled. In the back of her mind, the cynic in her was busy trying to find something—anything wrong with him. All she found was a man with creamy dark skin, intense brown eyes, and full, sensual lips.

There wasn't a damn thing wrong with this man.

"So how long have you been a firefighter?" she inquired, determined to fall for more than just his looks.

"Eighteen years," he boasted proudly, and then took a deep cleansing breath. "But I think it's finally over. Even if my ankle heals correctly, I don't think my career will ever be the same."

"What happened?"

"I was beaned by a huge chunk of ceiling. When I went down, my ankle folded like paper."

She winced. "I'm so sorry. Have you considered going into another division of the fire department?"

"None of them will give me that same rush of adrenaline, the same feeling of importance and making a difference."

She laughed. "You're starting to sound like my brother. It's a real judgment call on whether he's in it for the civil service or for the way the job elevates his testosterone."

The waiter returned with their drinks.

Lincoln laughed and reached for his glass of water. "Then we do have a lot in common. You said he lives in Decatur. Do you know what department he works out of?"

Peyton frowned as she tried to remember. "Sorry. Not off the top of my head. I'll have to ask him the next time I talk to him."

"Are you two ready to order?" Blake interrupted them with another charismatic smile.

"Sure," Lincoln said, reopening his menu. "I'll have a number thirty-four."

Peyton frowned. "You do know that foie gras is liver?"

Lincoln's handsome features twisted in disgust. "Uh, scratch that." He scanned the menu again.

"How about a twenty-three?" he asked, glancing over at Peyton.

She nodded. "A fancy cheeseburger."

"Perfect!" He beamed a bright smile up at the server as he handed over his menu.

"I'll have the same," she announced, charmed by her date's no-frills kind of attitude. "What happened to being adventuresome?"

"I call paying thirty dollars for a cheeseburger one hell of an adventure."

"Very well," the waiter snickered, and then disappeared from their table.

"So," Lincoln said, straightening in his chair. "What about you, Ms. P.J. Garner? Why don't you tell me a little about yourself—especially how you ended up with the name P.J.?"

"Well, P.J. is sort of a nickname. I found it also helped in business because so many people expected to meet a man when I went by my first name."

Lincoln's gaze caressed her face. "You look all woman to me."

"Why, thank you." Heat darkened the column of her neck.

"So what does it stand for—or am I not allowed to know?"

"I don't mind if you know," she said, shrugging. "It's Peyton. Peyton James Garner."

Chapter 11

"Are you all right, Lincoln?" Peyton reached across the table and squeezed his hand. "You look as though you've seen a ghost."

Lincoln forced the corners of his lips upward, but was unsure whether he'd mustered a smile. "Peyton is, uh, an unusual name for a woman. Probably not too many women are named . . . Peyton."

"Uh, probably . . . not." She laughed. "I didn't always like it growing up. The children were cruel, but I grew into it. When I started my agency, like I said, too many people had the false impression they were dealing with a man. I can't tell you how many times people thought I was my own secretary." She laughed. "So my ex-husband suggested that I start going by my nickname. It sounded more feminine. That way I would just bypass the initial confusion. It turns out to be the only thing he contributed to the relationship."

"Ouch."

She shrugged. "The truth hurts."

The meals arrived and Lincoln was unimpressed by the looks of his thirty-dollar cheese hamburger.

Peyton's cell phone rang. She made a quick apology and reached for her purse.

"Is there anything else I can get for you?" the waiter asked.

Lincoln cast a questioning look over at his date and then answered the waiter, "No. We're good."

"Very well."

"Michael." Peyton shook her head as she read the caller's ID. "No doubt Joey tattled that I had a date tonight. She's probably calling to see how it's going. Standard sister stuff. I'm just going to shut this off."

Michael and Joey? Lincoln smiled and rubbed at his temples. "So how *is* it going?" he asked, and then watched as her cheeks darkened prettily.

"I'm having a nice time."

"Good. So am I," he admitted, but then silence stretched uncomfortably between them. He tried to process what he'd just learned as he studied Peyton's angelic features.

"Peyton," he said, trying the name on for size. "You were saying that you were divorced?"

She sighed. "Yes, does that disappoint you?"

"No. No. Of course not." He reached for his glass of water and chugged it down with one gulp. "Garner. What is that—your maiden name?" he asked.

"No. It's Adams, actually."

Lincoln needed something stronger to drink.

Peyton rolled her eyes. "I know, I know. Why haven't I reverted to my maiden name?" she asked, and then proceeded to answer her own question. "Each week, month, and year I keep telling myself to get the paperwork started—but with the business and everything, it's more of a headache than anything else."

"Peyton Adams," he repeated for clarification.

She frowned. "Yes."

Too many thoughts raced through Lincoln's head. Number one concern was Flex's reaction to him dating his sister. Lincoln's eyes roamed over her again.

Flex's fine sister.

"Any children?" he asked, injecting warmth back into his voice.

"No. Neither one of us was ready for that."

"And now?"

She sucked in a stunned breath. "Maybe one day."

"Maybe?" He leaned in, grinning. "I've found that most women have made a decision on this matter somewhere around puberty."

"Are we gender-profiling again?"

He laughed and held up his hands. "You caught me. Sorry."

"Forgiven." She joined him in his silly grin. "But what about you?"

"Me?"

"Yeah, you. How many baby mamas do you have running around Atlanta?"

He nearly choked on his water. "None."

"That you're aware of," she challenged.

"Whoa, whoa. I don't have any rugrats circling the home front."

"Again—that you know of."

Fascinated by the way her eyes twinkled, Lincoln propped his elbows onto the white linen table and stared at her. "Okay. That I know of."

Peyton laughed and chalked one point for her on an invisible scoreboard. "You know, you also strike me as a man who loves to leave the toilet seat up."

"What?"

"You do, don't you?"

"I'm tired of women complaining about such nonsense," he said, laughing. "Learn to work the toilet seat. You're a big girl. If it's up, pull it down. We need it up. You need it down. You don't hear us complaining about you leaving it down." He smiled and gave himself one point.

"Uh-huh. I bet you watch sports all the time."

"And how many episodes of *Oprah* and *Dr. Phil* have you missed?" he retaliated.

"How do you handle arguments?" she challenged.

"I handle them fine as long as there's no crying and we're clear that anything I said six months ago is inadmissible. In fact, all comments become null and void after seven days."

"What?"

"Sounds perfectly fair to me."

"Can't handle tears? Not that I'm a crier."

He shrugged. "Crying is blackmail."

Sucking in a breath, she continued. "How are you about asking for directions when you're lost?"

"Christopher Columbus didn't need directions and neither do I. Just sit back and enjoy the scenery."

Peyton gave up and just started laughing. "At least you're honest."

"Speaking of gender-profiling," he said. "Not all men are interested in impregnating every woman they see—no matter how much fun it seems like on the surface."

Peyton giggled—damn it. *Well, it's certainly downhill from here.* "Let's make a deal," she said, lifting her glass of wine. "No more assumptions."

"Or judging," he added, raising his own glass. "For the rest of the night, we're going to approach every aspect of this relationship with an open mind."

Their glasses clinked together and then he took a hearty gulp.

"Relationship?" Peyton asked, after she had drained her glass. "That's sort of a big word—especially on a first date." Lincoln's dark gaze settled on her, while butterflies fluttered nervously in her stomach.

"Does the word terrify you?"

She hesitated.

"I'm going to take that as a yes. Now tell me why."

She cringed. "Why?"

"Yes. Help me understand you better."

His plea was more than tempting, it was downright seductive. Add that to the way he was looking at her, and she was pretty confident about the way this night would end. Giggling, butterflies, and a strong desire to see Lincoln Carver stripped naked and hovering over her were all signs that Peyton was a woman out of control.

"My family," she began, "places a lot of importance on marriage. Actually, at one time I did, too. In a family of six siblings, we all wanted what our parents had." A smile hugged her lips at the sudden memory of her parents dancing around the living room cheek to cheek.

"Their love was truly an inspiration. My two oldest sisters married replicas of our father, while the rest of us are hoping that we'll be just as fortunate. I, however, have the honor of being the first Adams to have gone through a divorce. It stings—and I guess it's easier to point fingers at the opposite sex than to entertain the notion that maybe the problem is you."

"So all this male bashing is like a defense mechanism."

Did she say that? "You're a fast learner," she whispered.

"Or . . . we have a lot in common," he suggested.

Peyton stared at him, once again loving everything her eyes graced upon. "Why aren't you married?" she asked suddenly. "At the stroke of midnight are you going to sprout another head or something?" Lincoln's rich bark of laughter wrung another smile from her.

"Nothing as dramatic as that, I assure you."

The waiter returned to the table and refilled their glasses and then slipped quietly away.

"I'm waiting," she prompted.

"Honestly, it's just been difficult to find the right woman, someone who accepts the dangers of being married to a firefighter, for one. Plus nice guys always finish last. Beneath my armor of confidence beats the heart of a regular Joe."

"And a budding artist."

"More like a closet artist. Up until a few months ago, I never showed anyone my work. It was just something I did in between home improvements."

Peyton's brows arched. "Home improvements? You mean like . . . repairing the roof or something?"

He laughed. "Yeah, or something."

"What do you know about cars?" she asked.

He frowned. "What do you mean?"

"Do you know how to fix a flat?"

"Yes."

"Oil change?"

"Afraid so."

"You know," she said, lifting her glass again, "I'm starting to think this is the beginning of a beautiful relationship."

"Has she made it back yet?" Michael inquired.

Groggy, Joey rolled over in bed and glanced at the digital clock. "Do you know what time it is?"

"Of course I do," Michael huffed impatiently. "Which is why I'm worried about her. What do we know about this guy she went out with anyway? Did you at least meet him?"

"No, I didn't meet him." Joey rubbed her eyes. "P.J. is a grown woman and more than capable of taking care of herself. This isn't exactly her first date."

"I think you should call the cops. New York is a scary place."

"How do you know? You've never been here."

"I watch the news."

"I'm hanging up," Joey warned, plopping her head back down onto a pillow. "I'll tell P.J. your news when she gets in or you can call back at a reasonable hour."

"Don't you dare hang up on me! Aren't you the least bit worried?"

"No. She met a nice guy and what she does with him is none of our concern. She's a grown woman."

"But—"

"Good night, Michael." Joey hung up and then rolled over in bed.

Under normal circumstances, a carriage ride through Central Park at one in the morning would have sounded a little suicidal to Peyton. However, taking the ride with Lincoln Carver had to be the most romantic thing she'd ever done.

"It's a full moon," Lincoln said, pointing up at the sky.

Her gaze followed his finger and settled on the large glossy orb hovering above them. "It's beautiful."

"Just like you," he whispered.

She cuddled closer, this time suppressing her girlish giggle. "It doesn't look so far away, does it?"

"No. It looks like you could just reach out and touch it," he agreed. His arm squeezed around her. "Would you like for me to lasso the moon for you?"

Peyton laughed. "And what would I do with my very own ball of dirt?"

"Hey, it was supposed to be romantic—lasso the moon, catch a falling star—you know, that sort of thing." He laughed along with her. "You wouldn't like any of that?"

Their eyes met through the glimmer of moonlight as she whispered, "I would much more prefer it if you would just kiss me again."

His deep, grooved dimples made another appearance. "A kiss? Is that all?"

When her gaze lowered to his full lips, she was hypnotized. "It'll do for now."

Lincoln's head descended in a slow arch and Peyton lifted her chin so she could meet him halfway. Nothing tasted as good as he did, nothing felt as liberating or as orgasmic as being wrapped in his embrace.

It can't be this easy, the devil on her shoulder whispered. However, Peyton had a hard time listening. She didn't want to think this through and she didn't want to question the emotions she was feeling.

And most importantly, she didn't want the night to end.

When their lips parted, Lincoln peppered a few extra kisses along her face and neck. She sighed with contentment and inched even closer. With her head pressed against his chest, she listened to the soft, melodious clicking of the horse trotting and enjoyed the caress of the early morning breeze.

"You know, this has turned out to be a pretty good night," she said. Her gaze once again centered on the full moon. "Maybe I was a little out of line when I attacked you this morning. You know, that whole bit about you being arrogant and not my type."

She drew a breath and a smile fluttered to her lips. "I hate to think I've turned into one of those bitter women who don't realize it." She chuckled. "What I'm saying is . . . I don't want this night to end."

When Lincoln didn't respond, she panicked and

rushed on. "I don't mean to sound forward or anything and I assure you I don't normally do this, but
I'd be lying if I said that I didn't feel this certain attraction to you . . . and I think that you feel it, too."

No answer.

Suddenly feeling foolish, Peyton pried herself out
of his arms. "Maybe we should just head on back. It's
getting pretty late."

Silence.

Frowning, Peyton glanced over at him and was
stunned speechless when she at last discovered that
Lincoln was sound asleep.

Chapter 12

Lincoln was out like a log.

Peyton tried everything to wake him, but was unable to wrest more than a few moans. "I don't believe this," she said, panting. Once she caught her breath, she reviewed her silly speech and laughed at the situation.

What was she supposed to do now? She'd no idea which hotel he was staying at, and it no longer seemed like a good idea to be roaming around Central Park at this ungodly hour.

"Driver, could you please take us to the Palace Hotel? I'll pay extra."

The man turned around and tipped his top hat to her.

Rolling her eyes and shaking her head at the heavens, Peyton asked why such things always seemed to happen to her. However, she couldn't quite make herself feel mad about the situation. Lincoln warned her he had mixed alcohol with his pain medication. However, as far as dating went, this night deserved a place in the record books.

At the Palace, it took three bellboys and one doorman to carry Lincoln up to Peyton's suite. When they arrived, they placed her large date on a Victorian sofa in the suite's living room.

She tipped the men generously, and then closed the door behind them. When she turned around, Joey bolted from the bedroom through the French doors.

"It's about time you made it back. Do you know what time—ohmigosh," she gasped when her gaze landed on Lincoln. She covered her scantily clad body with her hands and raced back through the doors. "I'm sorry, I didn't know you had company," she cried out.

Peyton laughed and wished she'd caught that performance on video. "It's okay," she said. "He's out cold." She removed Lincoln's jacket from her shoulder and draped it over a high-back chair.

The French doors slid open again and Joey peeked out. "What's he doing here?"

"He's my date." Peyton kicked off her shoes and headed over to the sofa.

Joey opened the door farther and timidly stepped through. This time she wore a gold satin robe. "Well, what the hell is wrong with him? What did you do?"

"Me?" Peyton sat on the end of the sofa and began removing Lincoln's shoes. "What makes you think I did something to him?"

"I don't know. The fact that he looks comatose might have something to do with it." Joey reached them and peered down at him. "You didn't slip something into his drink, did you? That's illegal, you know."

"Will you relax? I didn't do anything. He mixed some type of painkillers with alcohol and it knocked him out." She eased off one of his socks.

"Damn," Joey gasped. "That's a big foot." Her eyes

sparkled as they lifted and met Peyton's. "You know what they say about a man with big feet."

"Can it, Joey." She reached for his other leg. "I can do without the commentary."

"Hey, isn't he the guy you were freakin' at the club the other night?"

"The one and only."

"He was your date—he's your new artist?"

"I haven't decided if I'm going to represent him yet." Peyton stood and planted her hands on her hips as she stared down at him. He was actually adorable while he slept. Not to mention, he didn't snore. That was a major plus.

"Here, help me." Peyton leaned over and started undoing the buttons on his shirt. Seconds later, they peeled him out of it.

"Damn, is it getting hot in here?" Joey asked, fanning herself.

One look at Lincoln's muscled chest and Peyton felt the heat as well.

"Do you think there're any more where he comes from?" Joey asked.

"I don't know. I'm starting to think he's one of a kind." She reached for his belt. "Help me. No one sleeps in Armani."

"All right, this is where I draw the line." Joey held up her hands as she turned toward the French doors. "You're more than welcome to see your new boyfriend naked, I'm turning in."

"Come back here," Peyton huffed. "I need your help."

"Nope." Joey smirked. "But I will leave with a few pearls of wisdom: date rape is not the road you want to go down. Good night." She closed the doors.

"Smart-ass." Peyton rolled her eyes, and then refocused her attention on the man lying unconscious on the sofa. It took her more than twenty minutes to get him out of his pants and the one question she had all night was answered: he was a boxers man.

Housekeeping delivered an extra set of clean sheets, and in no time she had him all tucked in for the night. But before she retired, she found herself studying him while he slept.

He actually appeared to be grinning. Who was he thinking about? And were there legions of women waiting for him to return home? Probably.

She couldn't blame them. He was, hands down, the best kisser she'd ever had. Her gaze traced his face and then settled on his full lips. She remembered their intoxicating taste.

Peyton glanced at the French doors.

Temptation tugged at her and she took another glance at that beautiful mouth. *What would it hurt?*

She looked at the door again while her knees folded. *Just one little kiss. Surely, that would be okay.*

Her knees touched the carpet, while her eyes remained locked on his lips. "Well, Mr. Carver, I had a wonderful evening. Right up to the point where you fell asleep on me." She smiled. "Even then, you made it a night I'll never forget. But I have to tell you . . ." She leaned in close. ". . . You passed up on an opportunity for us to make beautiful music together."

As if he'd heard her, Lincoln sighed and snuggled deeper into the sheets.

"I would have rocked your world," she whispered. "You see, I do this amazing thing with my hips." Another long moan escaped him and a wider smile eased across her lips. She soaked in every detail of his features, determined not to forget a single line or plane that made him such a beautiful specimen.

"I would love to learn whatever tricks you have in your repertoire. Something tells me that kissing you is just the tip of the iceberg." She brushed the back of her hand along the side of his cheek. *So soft.*

"Good night, Lincoln." She leaned forward and pressed her lips against his. To her amazement, Peyton felt him return the kiss. She closed her eyes and allowed her world to spin out of control. If this was wrong, Lord, she didn't want to be right.

All too soon, the kiss ended and Lincoln drifted back to sleep.

Smiling, she stood up and turned off all the lights before she joined Joey behind the French doors. She tiptoed around quietly while she undressed.

Joey's sigh filled the room. "You're humming."

Peyton covered her mouth and then just as quickly lowered her hand. "Sorry," she said, and then climbed into bed still feeling giddy as a schoolgirl.

"By the way," Joey whispered, "I'm glad you finally kissed him."

Chapter 13

Yards of sapphire swirled inside Lincoln's head as well as the sound of an angel's laughter. He moaned as he stretched his body out as far as it would go before it snapped back contently beneath the covers.

"What a night, what a night," he groaned, but as he tried to recall specific details, he smacked into a mental roadblock.

There was the museum, the restaurant—Flex! His eyes bolted open. *P.J. is Peyton Adams—Flex's sister.* He sat up, but was immediately stunned by his surroundings. "Where in the hell am I?" He glanced around again, but nothing about the elaborate room triggered a memory.

"Oh, good morning. You're finally up."

Lincoln's head swiveled toward the French doors where Peyton sauntered through in a short satin robe. Those incredible legs strolled forward and hypnotized him on the spot.

"I was just about to make some coffee. Do you want some?"

What the hell happened last night? "I . . . huh?" He jumped, but was shocked to discover he was in his boxers. He fell back onto the sofa and scrambled to cover himself again. *No, I didn't. I didn't sleep with my buddy's sister.*

Peyton frowned. "Are you all right?"

"Fine, fine." He pulled the sheet up to his chin. "What, uh, where—what exactly happened last night?"

Her eyes sparkled as her lips curled up. "Don't tell me you don't remember."

One of her hands drifted seductively in front of her robe and Lincoln's gaze followed its slow descent. *Couldn't she do something with her hips?* As a lump swelled in his throat, he performed a series of coughs to try and clear it, but nothing was working.

"Did we, uh, you know—"

"Have sex?" she finished for him and lowered herself onto the cushion next to him.

Not trusting himself to speak, Lincoln bobbed his head and tensed in anticipation of her answer.

But she didn't respond; instead, her smile slid wider and she took her time crossing her sleek, toned legs.

"I think my, uh . . . medication and that champagne finally caught up with me and . . . what happened?"

Peyton rolled her eyes. "C'mon, don't play with me. You told me last night was the best night of your life."

"Oh, he's finally up?"

Lincoln's gaze jerked to another beauty standing in front of the French doors. She looked a lot like Peyton, maybe a few inches taller, and wore a short-cropped hairdo. The disturbing fact was that she, too, wore only a satin robe.

"So how did you sleep, lover boy?"

"You do remember Joey, don't you?" Peyton asked.

Lincoln felt light-headed. Surely, he didn't . . . wouldn't . . . not both of them.

"I don't think he remembers you, Joey." Peyton jabbed her fists into her hips.

Meanwhile, Joey fluttered a hand across her heart. "You have to be kidding me. And after all we did for him last night?"

"Goes to show you can never judge a book by its cover."

"Wait, wait." Lincoln stood up, but held the sheet around his body. "I apologize, ladies. It doesn't sound like I was at all myself last night. And I am *so* sorry. I wasn't thinking when I had that glass of champagne. Had I known it would produce this sort of side effect—"

"Lincoln—"

"I mean, not that any man wouldn't love to be with such beautiful women—"

"Linc—"

"It's just that . . . I don't usually—"

"Lincoln, nothing happened," Peyton blurted out.

He blinked, straightened, and then turned his confused expression toward Peyton. "But you just said—"

"April fools." She shrugged, and then laughed.

Joey joined in. "You should've seen your face. Priceless." She disappeared behind the French doors again.

Peyton stood and shrugged her shoulders. "I hope you're not mad, but I figured I owed you one for passing out on me last night."

Relieved beyond belief, Lincoln lowered himself back onto the sofa. "Oh, thank God." He exhaled and glanced around. "You wouldn't happen to know where my clothes are?"

"You're leaving?"

He clutched his sheet and noticed her wounded expression. "Well, I do . . . need to be heading back. I have some other things I need to take care of before I catch my flight tonight."

"You're going back to Atlanta tonight?"

"Afraid so," he whispered.

"I see." She broke eye contact and braided her hands together. "Well, it was certainly interesting meeting you."

Lincoln didn't want to end things with Peyton. He just wanted to get a permission slip first. "You're acting as if this is good-bye."

She folded her arms and struggled to put on a professional face. "Oh yeah. You're still looking for an agent."

He unwrapped the sheet from his body and stood before her in his boxers. "Yes. I still need an agent, but I don't think it's a wise idea that you and I work together."

"Why? I thought we've already been through this. I'm more than capable of separating business from my personal life."

"I believe you," Lincoln said simply, and closed the small distance between them. "But it's not you I'm worried about."

When his meaning dawned on Peyton, her cheeks darkened. He cupped her chin and tilted it up so their gazes met. "So, it's not good-bye, right?"

She swallowed and slowly shook her head.

"Good." He leaned forward and kissed her, but then he smiled against her lips at the sound of her gentle sigh. Flex was right again. Women who were tough as nails on the outside were soft and warm on the inside.

When her arms glided around his shoulders, Lincoln hardened at the feel of her breasts against his chest. He groaned and slid his hands down her curvy body.

"I see you two need to be alone."

Joey's interruption shattered the moment. Peyton and Lincoln jumped guiltily away from each other.

Peyton clutched at her robe. "We were, uh—"

"Uh, yeah, I was just leaving." Lincoln glanced around and spotted his clothes folded in a chair.

"No need. I'm heading out," Joey said, waltzing to the door. She had already dressed in a pair of blue jeans and a tight T-shirt with the slogan *got milk?* written across it.

Lincoln panicked. If he was left alone with Peyton, it would be too late to clear things with Flex. "I have to go, too." He snatched up his pants and hobbled while he put them on.

"You know, I can order up some breakfast," Peyton offered.

"Oh no. That won't be necessary." He slid on his shirt but didn't bother buttoning it. Shoes went on next, while socks were stuffed into his pockets.

"Are you sure? It shouldn't take—"

"Yeah, I'm sure." He grabbed his cane. "I'll call you," he said, bolting toward the door and fastening his pants as he went.

Joey jumped out of his way.

Lincoln snatched open the door and nearly collided into the housekeeper. "Sorry, ma'am." He turned again and flashed a smile at a stunned Peyton. "I swear, I'll call you."

Peyton blinked and he was gone.

"He's cute," Joey said, crossing her arms. "But there's definitely something strange about him."

Peyton couldn't agree more.

Chapter 14

After surviving a forty-eight-hour shift at Local 1492, Flex rewarded himself with a hot shower and a seaweed and cucumber facial mask. He could tell that his self-imposed mourning for his ten-year relationship was nearly at an end, because he was beginning to long for companionship.

Kicking back in his easy chair, while the soft soothing sounds of the ocean played on his stereo, Flex was just drifting off to sleep when the telephone rang.

Why didn't I unplug that thing?

The ringing continued, but he lacked the energy to get up and answer it. After a few more rings, the call was transferred to the answering machine.

"C'mon, c'mon. I know you're there." Michael's voice blasted through the speakerphone. "Pick up. There's something I have to tell you."

Flex groaned.

"If you don't pick up, I'm just going to hang up and call back."

Finally he got up. "Yeah, what is it?"

"Is that any way to talk to your older sister?" she

asked cheerfully. "Your sister who is getting married?"

Flex shrugged. "So what's new? You've been engaged for four years."

"Ha, ha. Keep that up and I won't invite you to my wedding in July."

"In three months?"

"Yes," she shrieked. "Can you believe it? We've finally set a date."

He blinked and stuttered for the right words. "That's great . . . and so soon."

"I know. The sooner the better, don't you think? I don't want to chance Phil selecting a date next year or something. Then I would've been engaged for *five* years and I'm just not going out like that."

Flex laughed. "Well, this is great. Congrats!"

"You're coming, right?"

"Ooh," he said, cringing. "With it being short notice—"

"Francis Marion Adams, you swore when you left here you'd come back for my wedding and you better believe I'm holding you to that."

"All right, all right. I'll be there. What's the date?"

"July Fourth."

"Starting the marriage off with a bang," he laughed.

"Just another reason to celebrate. Plus, this way Phil won't be able to forget our anniversary."

"If you say so." Flex returned to his armchair and kicked his feet up. "Fourth of July, I got it."

"Great. Try to show up a few days early so everyone can play catch-up with you."

"Will do." He yawned.

"And don't forget to bring that handsome new boyfriend of yours Peyton told us about."

Flex sat up. "Huh?"

"Trey Carver. Isn't that his name? Boy, the whole family can't wait to meet him. Even Dad."

"Dad?"

"Oh boy, Flex. You would be so proud of him. He's really trying to come around and understand this whole alternative lifestyle thing."

"I'm gay, Michael, not Chinese."

"C'mon. You know what I mean. He loves you and he's trying his best. Give him a chance."

Flex sighed.

"What better way for him to understand you than for him to meet the new love of your life?"

"Uh, about Trey—"

"I'm also looking forward to meeting him. I hope he's able to pass the 'sisters' test.' " She laughed. "But I'm sure he'll be fine."

"Trey's not going to be able to come."

"Why not?"

"Well, it *is* short notice. We both can't just . . . you know, just up and leave."

"You haven't even asked him."

"I don't have to ask. You know how it is in a department. Our schedules rarely allow us time together, let alone allow time for both of us to fly across the country. It will be difficult enough for just me to get the time off," he lied.

She fell silent for a moment. "Then maybe we should bring the wedding to you?"

Michael was crazy enough to do just that. "No, no. That's way too much trouble. I'll talk to him. I'm sure we'll be able to work something out."

"Are you sure? I mean, it'll be more expensive if we come out there, but I'm sure I can get everyone to agree. We've all been dying to come out and visit anyway."

"No, no. I won't put the family through that kind of inconvenience. We'll be there."

"You promise?"

He winced and dropped his head into the palm of hand. "Yeah, I promise."

"Fifty bucks he doesn't call." Peyton slammed her clothes into her new suitcase. Anger was the only thing that prevented her from crying. "Not that I care."

"If he doesn't, then to hell with him," Joey huffed, plopping down on her bed while she watched Peyton pack. "I thought we weren't leaving until tomorrow."

"There's no crime in getting ready early, is there?" she snapped.

"No. Not at all." Joey held up her hands. "I'm surprised you're so upset. It was just *one* date. Yeah, he's cute and all, but—"

"Who said I was upset? I don't care if he *ever* calls."

"Uh-huh." Joey folded her legs so she could sit Indian style. "For someone who didn't get laid, you sure are showing signs of being sprung."

"I'm not sprung." Peyton dropped to her knees and searched under the bed for a missing pump.

"If he calls—not that you care whether he does or not—will you go out with him again?"

Peyton stopped. "I don't know. I'd have to think about it."

"Oh boy. You really do have it bad."

"Look, I'm not going to lie and say I had a terrible time last night."

"Even though he fell asleep on you?"

"It wasn't his fault, he mixed alcohol with his medication—"

"And he ran out of here like you told him you were having his kid."

"What—are you getting off on this or something?" Peyton snapped. "Fine, I'm a little hurt. I admit it."

The room fell silent before Joey responded, "Sorry, P.J."

Peyton sighed and climbed up onto the bed. "I can't believe it. The first guy that stimulates my mind and gives me butterflies just blew me off like I was contagious."

Joey switched beds so she could drape a supportive arm around her sister. "Maybe there is a perfectly good reason why he acted the way he did. And who knows? He might call you."

Peyton rolled her eyes. "Please. 'I'll call you' is the universal brush-off line. I should know. I've used it religiously." She moaned and fell back against the bed.

"Poor thing."

Joey stroked her hair for a few minutes and Peyton was beginning to enjoy their small pity party. "Don't get offended or anything, but you didn't get on a soapbox or anything on your date, did you?"

"What do you mean?"

Joey sighed. "Well, you know how you get. You start preaching about things you don't like about men—they watch too much sports or they don't know how to listen—and don't forget how much you don't care for metrosexual men."

Peyton grew uneasy. "We both . . . discussed the difference between the sexes."

"I'm going to take that as a yes."

She sat up. "What's wrong with that? He had his own list as well."

"Great. There're two of you."

"That's what I'm saying. We had a lot in common. And believe me, it's refreshing to meet a guy with honest observations about the dating scene."

Joey groaned and shook her head. "There is such a thing as being too honest, P.J. How many times do I have to tell you men don't want to hear what they're doing wrong? It's a major turnoff."

"It's wasn't like that," Peyton assured her, though

she was really trying to convince herself. Had she blown it?

Joey stroked Peyton's hair while silence filled the space between them. "Michael called last night."

"Oh, please tell me you didn't tell her that I was out on a date."

"You didn't tell me not to," Joey said defensively.

"Great. Now I'm going to be grilled by Curly, Larry, and Moe."

"I don't think it's going to be that bad. She has other news that should take her mind off your love life for a while."

Peyton sat up. "I can't imagine that. What is it?"

"Believe it or not—"

The phone rang.

"That's probably her now." Joey reached over to the nightstand and picked up the phone. "Hello." She rolled her eyes.

Peyton shook her head and waved for Joey to tell her sister that she wasn't there.

"Yes, Michael. She's right here." Joey handed her the phone and whispered, "I had to talk to her all last night. It's your turn."

Peyton sighed and grabbed the phone. "Hello, Mike. What's up?"

"I should ask you that question," Michael said sweetly. "What's this I hear about you being out all night?"

"Just having some fun. Nothing serious." Peyton pinched the bridge of her nose. "I hear you have some good news?"

"Yep. I need for you and Joey to head back home and help me prepare for my *wedding*."

"You've set a date?" Peyton said with disbelief.

"Can you believe it? It's going to be on July Fourth. We're going to have it at Dad's house and I've already talked to Flex. He and his boyfriend Trey are coming down, so there's no need for you to go to Atlanta. I need you here."

"Three months? That's not a lot of time."

"Hey, there's nothing the Adams family can't do. So hurry up and get your butt back here. And when you get here I want to hear all about this date of yours."

"Just call him already," Tyrone said, cramming on his Yankees hat. "The worst he could do is kill you for banging his sister."

"Nothing happened," Lincoln said as he poured himself a cup of coffee. "That pain medication knocked me out."

"Says you." Tyrone winked.

"That's my story and I'm sticking to it."

"Well, I wouldn't be going around boasting that I fell asleep on a beautiful woman. Trust me. It's not going to win you any playa points with the guys."

"I'm not interested in being a playa." He lowered himself into a cramped chair. "By the way, you should see the rooms over at the Palace. They look like high-rise condominiums. We need to stay there next time."

"Sure. Just as soon as my rich uncle gets out of the poorhouse. Of course, if you become this big-time artist, then we can stay anywhere you like. But I have to tell you, if your girl can afford to stay at the Palace, then she must be pulling down some serious cheese."

"I'm not bothered by a woman making more money than I am." Lincoln shrugged. "In fact, I find it a bit of a turn-on. A woman who can hang with the big boys by day and then purr with me at night? What's not to love?"

"Purr? You know how to make a woman purr?"

"Can we please focus? What if Flex flips when I tell him I want to date his sister? When I inquired about his sisters before, he just brushed me off—like it was taboo or something."

Tyrone nodded and crossed his arms as he considered Lincoln's point. "I guess it would be in bad taste to screw over a guy who saved your life."

"Exactly."

"Then again, you could always act like you didn't know it was his sister. Peyton Garner—Peyton Adams. It could be an honest mistake. You might be sweating over nothing. One date doth not a relationship make, my friend."

"Yeah, but I'd feel better if I had my man's permission."

Tyrone snatched up the phone and held it out. "Then stop talking about it and call him."

Chapter 15

"Leave me alone," Flex moaned at the ringing phone, and then buried his head farther beneath the pillows. He cursed himself again for not shutting off the ringer or, better yet, yanking the cord out of the wall.

The ringing continued until he remembered that when it came to his sisters, resistance was futile.

"Make it quick," he croaked into the receiver.

"Flex?"

Frowning, he tried to place the voice. "Yeah, who's this?"

"It's Linc, man. Did I catch you at a bad time?"

"Pulled a straight forty-eight, so make it quick."

Lincoln cleared his throat. "Nah, I think this can wait. You go ahead and get some sleep. I'll just holler at you when I get back into town."

"I'm awake now. Spill it."

"Really, it's—"

"I take it this has something to do with your date last night?"

Silence greeted his question.

"Don't tell me you crashed and burned."

"Oh, never that, man. Never that. I, uh, just wanted to swing out this hypothetical situation at you."

"Hit me." Flex yawned and sank deeper in the sheets.

"A friend of mine . . . well, you know how sometimes we as boys don't like it when our buddies start dating an ex-girl or . . . family member—you know, cousins, sisters, aunts, or what have you?"

"I think so, yeah," Flex said, slowly drifting off to sleep.

"Well, have you ever had a situation when one of your boys wanted to date . . . you know, one of your family members?"

"One of my 'boys'?" Flex chuckled lazily. "That would *never* happen. Wait, I did have an old high school buddy that dated one of my sisters. Big mistake."

"Oh." Lincoln cleared his throat. "Well, let's just say that you were interested in Henry's, ah, sister."

"I didn't know he had a sister."

"Yeah, she's a nice girl."

"All right."

"So anyway, you like his sister and you two go out a few times. You don't tell Henry because he'll nut up if he found out. So—"

"Linc, if you care about this woman, see her. It's an A-and-B relationship. Keep Henry out of it, but both of you must agree to that. If it develops into something serious, the only thing that's going to matter to Henry is that you make his sister happy. If it doesn't work out just make sure that you and Henry's sister part on good terms."

"After a long pause, Lincoln admitted, "That's pretty deep."

"Well, I do what I can. Now I'm going back to sleep."

"Cool, cool. I'll catch up with you later," Lincoln

said, and ended the call. That was much harder than he had expected.

"So what did he say?" Tyrone asked, popping peanuts into his mouth.

Lincoln glanced up and frowned. "You know that stuff in the minibar costs, don't you?"

"Yeah, yeah. I got it. How much could it possibly be?" He laughed. "Now tell me what he said."

Lincoln smiled and pushed up on his cane. "I would love to, but I have to go. There's someone I have to see first." He winked. "Wish me luck."

Peyton flipped through the pages of Lincoln's portfolio while the director of the Museum of African Modern Art briefed her over the phone about the success of last night's show. However, five minutes into the conversation, Peyton's attention had drifted. She was too busy trying to imagine Lincoln in the throes of creating one of his pieces. Of course, flights of fancy had him welding with nothing but a pair of boxers on.

A warm tingle coursed through her body as she remembered what those large chiseled muscles looked like. Why couldn't they have been alone this morning? Why did he have to fall asleep last night?

"Ms. Garner, are you still there?"

"Yes, Mary. I'm here. Uh, thanks for calling with those numbers. You and your staff were phenomenal. I know I'm looking forward to the next time we work together." She smiled and added more small talk before she finally ended the call.

While Joey was out shopping again, Peyton dove into work, making one phone call after another and pretending that she was already over Mr. Lincoln Carver.

"It's just lust," she mumbled under her breath.

"He's a good-looking man, a great kisser—and damn it, why didn't he want me?" She tossed down her pen and flopped back in her chair.

Not that she was conceited or anything, but she looked damn good last night. Hell, she would have hit on herself if— "Okay, I'm losing it now."

She drew a breath and released it in a long exhale. What was she going to do now? She'd already finished packing for tomorrow, her heart wasn't into working, and she didn't feel like shopping—that was a miracle in itself.

Maybe the best thing to do was to find the nearest ice cream shop and load up on some chocolate. She'd think about hitting the dating scene once she returned home.

At the loud knock on the door, she frowned and searched her memory for a forgotten appointment. She pushed out of her chair just as the knock grew persistent.

"Who is it?" she asked, and then peered through the peephole.

There was no one there.

Confused, she opened the door, but then jumped when an arm jutted out, and in its hand was a long-stem rose.

Peyton gasped and then reached for it.

"I figured it would be a nice start to make up for last night."

She turned toward the sound of Lincoln's voice. "I thought you left," she whispered in surprise.

Lincoln stepped forward and consumed her senses. "I made a slight change in plans. I hope you don't mind."

"Why would I mind?" she asked. Her heartbeat raced and those wonderful butterflies returned to swarm her insides. "Would you like to come in?"

"I would rather we went out." He took her hand in his and brought it up to his lips. "Maybe even finish our date where we left off?"

"A ride through Central Park?"

"For starters." He backed her against the door frame. "And then afterward, perhaps we could—"

"Go dancing?" she suggested.

"Actually, I think I have to retire my dancing shoes. At least for a little while." His head descended so that his warm breath brushed against her face. "I'm glad I came back to see you."

She lifted her gaze and when she met his intense stare everything melted inside her. "Kiss me," she whispered.

Without question he did just that. He kissed her with a fierce passion that she met and matched, while his hands drifted down her back and hips. When that wasn't enough he pulled her close and molded her body against his.

Peyton emitted another weak moan at the feel of his hard body pressed against her. The length of his arousal increased her body's endorphins.

She didn't know what made him change his mind and she didn't care. All that mattered was he was here. They moved farther into the room and Lincoln kicked the door closed.

When the kiss ended, her eyes remained closed, while her mind drifted somewhere among the clouds. "I'm glad you came back, too," she said.

Lincoln smiled. "You should grab a jacket."

What was he talking about? She was burning up and she wanted nothing more than to relieve both of them of their clothes or to at least slip her hands beneath his shirt and enjoy the feel of his spectacular abs and mountainous chest.

The door bolted open.

"P.J., I found the perfect thing to cheer you up." Joey looked up from her shopping, and then jumped back.

Peyton and Lincoln stared wide-eyed at their intruder.

Joey smiled. "I see you found something better to cheer you up."

Lincoln disbursed a hearty laugh. "Hello again."

"What are you doing back here?" Peyton asked. At this rate she was never going to get laid.

Joey started backing up to the door. "Hey, I know when I'm not wanted. I'll leave you two alone."

Lincoln shook his head. "That won't be necessary. We were just leaving."

"We were?"

He looked down at her. "Central Park, remember?"

What's the hurry? "Yeah, sure." She glanced back at her sister and gave her a tight smile. "He's right. We were just leaving."

Joey suppressed her laughter, but her face glowed a bright cranberry red. "You two have fun."

Peyton stood and mumbled as she walked past her sister. "We were until you showed up."

"Back again?"

Lincoln smiled up at the same carriage driver from last night. "Everything's better the second time around," he boasted with a wink.

"I just might have to hold you to that," Peyton whispered in his ear.

"By all means." He opened the carriage door and assisted her inside. When he took his place beside her, he slid his arm around her shoulder.

There was something about this woman that he just couldn't get enough of. He wanted to talk more so they could really get to know each other. Yet at the same time, talk was the last thing he wanted to do.

Pace yourself, pace yourself. One of the major things he'd learned from his past relationships was that there was such a thing as too much too fast; and he was more than aware that he and Peyton were in danger of doing just that.

Of course it would be nice to see what she'd look like in the heat of passion—maybe even to hear if she'd call out his name in the throes of ecstasy.

"What are you thinking about?" she asked.

"Things I shouldn't be thinking about," he admitted honestly.

"Why don't you tell me and let me decide?"

He smiled at the sudden glint in her eyes and looked away. She was a strong woman who was unquestionably comfortable in her own skin and her sexuality.

Peyton's fingers directed his chin downward so he would meet her gaze again. "You can tell me. I won't bite."

Easily seduced by her silky tone, Lincoln found it difficult to censor his words, like his relationship guru had taught, and spoke from his heart.

"I'm wondering about what you'd look like while I make love to you."

"You didn't have to wonder about that, you know." She chuckled. "You could've found out last night— or this morning."

Lincoln blinked in surprise.

Peyton turned her head so her lips brushed against his ear. "You should see all the things I can do to you."

Erotic images filled his head, each one better than the last. *Pace yourself, pace yourself.*

"I'm sure it will be wonderful when the time is

right." His reply had the effect of splashing cold water on the idea. "You know—after we get to know each other better."

She blinked and stared at him as though a second head had sprouted from his neck.

Flex had warned that he would get this initial reaction. But he'd told Lincoln that such restraint was often viewed as a challenge by women. Besides, the last thing he wanted was to be nothing more than a weekend affair to this beautiful businesswoman—a course she seemed determine to set them on.

Finally, a slow smile returned to her lips. "And when do you think the time *will* be right?"

Now. "What's your hurry?" he asked. "Are you looking for Mr. Right or for Mr. Right Now?" He leaned back. "I have to tell you, I'm looking for Mrs. Right."

She was adorable with her scrunched-up nose and furrowed brow. "Mrs. Right?" she repeated.

"Yeah, you know, the whole one-man-for-one-woman thing?"

"Mrs. Right?" She glanced around at the people they passed in the park.

"What's wrong?"

"Nothing. I'm just expecting *Candid Camera* or something to jump out of the bushes."

Lincoln snickered. "Why is this so hard to believe?"

"Do you know what the chances are of running into a guy like you who is *honestly* looking to settle down?"

"It's not as rare as you think. Men have different ways of going about finding the right person. But in the end we're all looking for the same things—something to do, something to look forward to, and someone to love."

She stared at him. "I don't know if I believe you.

What are you, hooked up to a machine that makes you say all the right things?"

Laughing, he turned his gaze to take in their surroundings. "Actually, I'm an old-fashioned man who's tired of all the games. We both know that if we meet on a Saturday and sleep together on Sunday, the chances of us being together next week, next month are slim to none. I've already given up the opportunity for you to represent me for a chance at a relationship. I'm not willing to forsake a lifetime for a few hours of sex."

She swallowed. "A few hours?"

Lincoln glanced at her. "At least." He smiled. "You still haven't told me what you're looking for."

Peyton rolled her eyes. "Honestly? It's a pretty long list."

He shrugged. "I can't think of a better time to review it."

The glint returned to her eyes and a sexy smile to her lips. "All right then. I'm looking for a old-fashioned kind of man."

"Check."

"Let me finish," she said, holding up her hands. "This man must know the difference between a Phillips head and a Reed-and-Prince head screwdriver."

"Check." Lincoln crossed his arms. "I'm looking for a woman who knows how to use the stove instead of a microwave."

"Check." She smiled smugly. "I want a man who knows how to do a standard oil change, fix a flat, and rotate the tires on a car."

"Check, check, and check." He matched her smile. "How about a woman who knows how to use a vacuum cleaner?"

"You're looking for a wife or a mother?"

"I'm looking for the mother of my children," he responded.

"Children?" she asked.

"Yes, children. How do you feel about them?"

"I, uh, feel okay. Especially when I know that they're going home with someone else."

His heart dropped in disappointment. "You don't want kids?"

Peyton glanced away. "It's not that I don't want them, it just that I've never allowed myself to think about the possibility."

"But you were married before."

"The whole thing was a mistake. I hate to admit that I was once one of those women who married for the sake of being married, but I was. Ricky never expressed an interest in children and neither did I. Once I graduated from college, I assumed the next step was marriage and took the first man who asked me. How pathetic is that?"

"And now?"

She grinned at the idea, a small boy with Lincoln's dimples. "Now . . . I'm thinking about it."

Chapter 16

Peyton enjoyed the rest of her ride through Central Park cuddled next to Lincoln. Despite her many visits to the busy city, she'd never taken the time to tour the park's lush rolling meadows.

It was a beautiful day for falling in love and that was exactly what Peyton feared she was doing. This was a far cry from her morning of sexual frustration. Now, as she sat next to what was arguably her dream guy, her mind played Photoshop with images of their future children. Children. How pathetic.

She loved every minute of it, and the day didn't stop there.

An early dinner was in the glorious Crystal Room at Tavern on the Green. While Peyton was no stranger to fine dining, it was apparent that Lincoln was stretching out of his comfort zone again to show her a good time—and she was charmed by it.

However, the pessimist in her kept waiting for the bubble to burst. No man could meet her every expectation, but as dinner wore on she was beginning to believe that maybe, just maybe, there was one.

"So what happens after tonight?" she asked.

"What do you mean?"

Peyton gently stirred her bowl of lobster bisque, while choosing the right words. "Well, tomorrow I return to California and you're going back to Georgia."

"True." He drew a deep breath and exhaled it slowly. "A lot has happened this weekend."

"Yeah. It's a shame that it has to end."

"Why is that?"

"Well . . . to be honest with you, I've never had a long-distance . . . relationship. I mean, I have friends who've tried their hands at it, but I'd be hard pressed to name a couple who was successful."

"So what you're telling me is that we'll be the first?"

His response surprised her. "There goes that cocky streak again."

"Is cocky a step up from arrogant?"

"I guess you could say that." She smiled and found it difficult to erect her old, familiar walls of defense, and as the night wore on she stopped trying.

"What makes you so sure we have what it takes to make this last?"

"Intuition."

"More like wishful thinking?"

"What's wrong with that?" He searched her gaze. "It's not exactly healthy to enter into a new relationship expecting it to fail. If you're going to do that, why bother?"

Peyton swallowed. "You know it's going to take me a while to get used to a man who tosses the R-word around like it's nothing."

"Does it make you nervous?"

Their waiter suddenly appeared and refreshed their drinks, which allowed Peyton sufficient time to come up with a good response.

"It takes a lot to make me nervous."

An Important Message From The ARABESQUE Publisher

Dear Arabesque Reader,

I invite you to join the club! The Arabesque book club delivers four novels each month right to your front door! It's easy, and you will never miss a romance by one of our award-winning authors!

With upcoming novels featuring strong, sexy women, and African-American heroes that are charming, loving and true… you won't want to miss a single release. Our authors fill each page with exceptional dialogue, exciting plot twists, and enough sizzling romance to keep you riveted until the satisfying end! To receive novels by bestselling authors such as Gwynne Forster, Janice Sims, Angela Winters and others, I encourage you to join now!

Read about the men we love… in the pages of Arabesque!

Linda Gill
PUBLISHER, ARABESQUE ROMANCE NOVELS

*P.S. Watch out for the next Summer Series **"Ports Of Call"** that will take you to the exotic locales of Venice, Fiji, the Caribbean and Ghana! You won't need a passport to travel, just collect all four novels to enjoy romance around the world! For more details, visit us at www.BET.com.*

THE "THANK YOU" GIFT INCLUDES:

- 4 books absolutely FREE (plus $1.99 for shipping and handling).
- A FREE newsletter, *Arabesque Romance News*, filled with author interviews, book previews, special offers, and more!
- No risks or obligations. You're free to cancel whenever you wish with no questions asked.

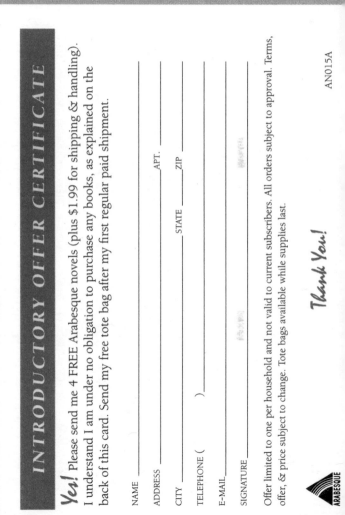

INTRODUCTORY OFFER CERTIFICATE

Yes! Please send me 4 FREE Arabesque novels (plus $1.99 for shipping & handling). I am under no obligation to purchase any books, as explained on the back of this card. Send my free tote bag after my first regular paid shipment.

NAME _____

ADDRESS _____ APT. _____

CITY _____ STATE _____ ZIP _____

TELEPHONE ( ) _____

E-MAIL _____

SIGNATURE _____

Offer limited to one per household and not valid to current subscribers. All orders subject to approval. Terms, offer, & price subject to change. Tote bags available while supplies last.

AN015A

Thank You!

ARABESQUE

THE ARABESQUE ROMANCE CLUB: HERE'S HOW IT WORKS

THE ARABESQUE ROMANCE BOOK CLUB
P.O. BOX 5214
CLIFTON NJ 07015-5214

PLACE
STAMP
HERE

"That doesn't answer my question."

It doesn't?

Lincoln leaned back in his chair while his Cheshire Cat smile slid wider. "Never mind. I think I already have my answer."

Peyton tensed. His twinkling gaze somehow stripped her of whatever was left of her defenses, and trying to acclimate to this new sense of vulnerability was frightening.

"I like the fact that I make you nervous," he said. "It means you're scared of losing control."

"And that's supposed to be a good thing?" When his warm gaze caressed her face, she marveled over what he could do without laying a finger on her.

Lincoln leaned forward once again. "If it makes you feel any better," he whispered, "I'm a little nervous myself."

She searched his eyes for sincerity and then smiled when she found it. "Then why don't you look as terrified as I feel?"

"I think the word is *excited.*"

"You say tomato and I say—"

"You really need to work on this pessimistic thing you have going."

"And you have to do something about this eternal sunshine thing."

He laughed. "So do you think you can fall in love with a guy you can't stand?"

"We'll just have to see."

"She went out with the same man again?" Michael belted into the phone. "Who is this guy, anyway?"

Joey rolled her eyes and continued packing her things. "Don't worry about it. It's no one you know."

"I know lots of people. Besides, if Peyton actually

has the nerve to see someone more than once, then this a monumental event and the family should be informed."

"C'mon, Michael. We're not the Mafia. I'm sure she dates plenty of men more than once. She's just smart enough not to tell us about it."

"Name one."

"Ricky Garner."

"Don't be a smart-ass," Michael hissed. "I'm not talking about ancient history."

Laughing, Joey plopped onto the bed. She gave up trying to figure out how to cram six shopping bags of new clothes into luggage that was already jammed tight. "Let it go, Mike. When she wants the *family* to know who she's dating, she'll tell us."

"You know."

"Leave me out of it. I see, hear, and know nothing. Besides, it's probably not even serious. You know how P.J. can be. He's probably just someone to pass the time with in New York. Drop it."

"There's something you're not telling me. How could you hold out on your older sister?"

"You mean my nosey sister. Don't you have wedding crap you have to get through?"

"Fine. Don't tell me, but don't think I won't remember this."

Joey looped the phone cord around her neck and pretended to hang herself. Michael was like an elephant when it came to remembering things.

"But you're right," Michael added. "Peyton has way too much armor to get into anything serious. Forget I asked."

Joey exhaled.

"But you're still not off the hook."

"Of course not."

* * *

Peyton and Lincoln laughed and talked for hours after their dinner plates were removed from the table. There was a wealth of things to do in the city that never sleeps, but the couple didn't want to do any of them, nor did they want the night to end.

To prolong their time together, they took in a Broadway play, and then a long leisurely walk among the glorious lights of Times Square. It was another beautiful night and the air was ripe for romance.

"So you're an only child?" Peyton asked, shaking her head. "I can't imagine life without my crazy siblings."

Lincoln's chest rumbled with a quiet laughter. "It would've been nice to have a younger brother to boss around, play practical jokes on, or even frame for some of my misdeeds."

"Misdeeds? Were you a rebel without a cause, Mr. Carver?"

"Afraid so." He sighed. "As a teenager I would do anything to get my father's attention." He fell silent for a moment. "It always seemed like everything else was more important than me. Long hours at the fire station meant no time for Saturday football games or going to the zoo. Hell, his cars were even more important. I can't tell you how many times I hated watching him wash and wax his beloved Bessie."

"Bessie?"

"He named all his cars Bessie." He chuckled. "I have no idea why."

She frowned. "What is your relationship with your father like now?"

"Strained, but better. He's been able to open up over the years. In the end, I think he's just a man who'd seen too much in his life. Mom said it stemmed back to Vietnam, but he never talks about it. Looking at it now, I'm convinced he did the best he could."

The snapshot image of his childhood made a

strong impression on Peyton. She even felt guilty for having the opposite experience.

"What about you?" he asked.

She closed her eyes. "My parents were great. They never argued in front of us, I never felt they loved one more than the other, but my world was forever shaken when my mother passed away."

Lincoln's arm tightened around her shoulder as he whispered, "I'm so sorry."

A dull ache throbbed around her heart, but she lifted her chin and braved a smile. "It's okay. You know, it's true what they say about time healing all wounds." She paused. "The thing that made me angry about her passing was that it was preventable."

"How—"

"Ovarian cancer," she said quietly. "See, Mom didn't believe in doctors. Now, if *we* got a paper cut, we were rushed to the nearest hospital. But when it came to taking care of herself, she didn't have the time." She closed her eyes at the feel of his lips pressed against her forehead and reveled in the security his arms offered.

Oh yes. He's a keeper.

"How come you don't talk about your job that much?" Peyton asked, switching gears. "Most firefighters I know talk of little else."

"Then I can't possibly tell you anything you don't already know." He chuckled. "Besides"—he tapped his ankle with his cane—"I have to start embracing the idea of embarking on a new career."

"You still have a lot of options."

"True. And I'm sure no matter what I decide to do I'll be great at it."

Peyton glanced up at him.

"Too much confidence again?"

She smiled. "It's all right. I'm starting to like it."

He jiggled his eyebrows in a Groucho Marx fashion. "I'm making progress."

I'd say. Peyton smiled. Everything was happening too fast and normally she was too much of a cynic to be falling for any of it.

Both fell silent and just enjoyed the sights and sounds around them. Soon, the lights were behind them and her hotel quickly came into view. It was time to say good-bye again.

"You're pretty close to your siblings, aren't you?" he asked out of the blue.

"Pretty much. We do tend to get on each other's nerves every once in a while, but that's pretty normal."

"Yeah, I'm sure it is." He drew a breath. "Have you ever dated a friend of, say, your brother?"

Peyton laughed aloud. "Oh, God, yes. Worst mistake of my life."

"R-really?" He cleared his throat.

"The first boy I'd ever kissed was in Flex's Boy Scout troop. I thought it was a magical experience until I'd later learned he told the whole neighborhood that we did more than just kiss. When my brother found out, he made a point to beat the guy up every day after school for like a month. Flex also got expelled, but he got his point across."

"He's really protective?"

"Very—even though he's the baby of the family."

Lincoln nodded as they walked. "But that was a long time ago."

"Then there was a time in junior high when I went to the prom with his friend, Tanner Beckham. Except I wasn't the only one Tanner brought to the prom. He was the first playa who played me."

He made a face. "Junior high, huh?"

"Then in high school, I met Ricky Garner."

Lincoln exhaled. "So, basically, it hasn't worked out for you?"

"That's putting it mildly. I swore I would never date any friends, coworkers, or neighbors of any of my siblings—and let me tell you, that's a long list." She glanced up at him as they entered the hotel. "Why do you ask?"

He shrugged. "No reason."

Their steps slowed as they walked across the spacious lobby to the elevator bay. It was the end of a beautiful day . . . and quite possibly the end of their time together. It was a little late, but Peyton glanced at his hand in search of a ring. When she didn't see one or an impression of one, she relaxed—but only a little.

They'd reached her floor all too soon, with Peyton grappling with how she was going to morph this budding friendship into something more.

"Well, here we are." She glanced up at him. "Would you like to come in for a nightcap?" she asked, but as Lincoln drew in a deep breath, she knew his answer.

"How about a rain check?"

She fought off her disappointment and embarrassment with little success. "Sure. That will be fine." Peyton stepped back to put some distance between them and for her to maintain her composure.

Lincoln, however, stepped forward and continued to dominate her senses. "Have you ever been to Savannah?"

Peyton blinked. "Georgia?"

He nodded. "There is this beautiful place on Tybee Island I go to once a year. It's where I go for inspiration." His smile sloped. "It's not California, but you won't find any fault with the beach or the laid-back southern living."

"Is this an invitation?" Her body warmed to the spark of hope.

His eyes lowered to her lips. "I believe it is."

"When?"

"Next weekend."

She sucked in a breath. "The wedding."

He chuckled. "Boy, talk about moving fast."

"Not us." Peyton popped him lightly on the arm. "My sister Michael. She's getting married this July. On top of running a business, I'm sure whatever free time I do have will be devoted to her wedding preparations."

"Oh well. If you can't come, I understand."

"No," she decided suddenly. "I want to go. It'll probably take me a few days to iron out the details, but count me in."

"Great." Lincoln edged closer and slid an arm around her waist. "How about a kiss to seal the deal?" Without hesitation, he tilted her chin, met her gaze, and leaned in for a kiss.

While her head filled with clouds and her body with butterflies, Peyton tried not to get caught up in the moment. While he wasn't the first good-looking man she'd gone out with, he was the first to ignore her sexual advances. Maybe that was what intrigued her. What woman wouldn't respond to such a challenge?

It won't last.

Her body trembled as the kiss deepened, and her arms slid effortlessly around his neck. Even still, the cynic within her remained.

The weekend may have been perfect, but soon, she told herself, this prince would turn into a frog—they always did.

Chapter 17

For three months, Lincoln occupied his time sculpting, seeking an agent, avoiding Flex, and spending long hours in pillow talk with his new lady love. They had taken a couple of romantic trips to Savannah and Las Vegas as well in the last few months. He believed wholeheartedly that Peyton Garner was his soul mate.

"I think you should've hit it when you had the chance," Tyrone commented, as he set out the deck of playing cards and a tray of poker chips.

"Haven't you heard of 'too much, too fast'?" Lincoln asked, grabbing a few bottles of beer from the refrigerator. "Besides, this is Flex's sister. A man should definitely show a little more respect."

"Personally, I think Flex is turning you into a pansy." Tyrone sat down at the table and started counting the cards to make sure he had a full deck. "Carriage rides, expensive dinners, and no sex are all signs of trouble. You need to come back to the playa side of things."

"I've been on that side before and it's never gotten

me anywhere. I'm going to do the right thing this time—no matter how many cold showers I have to take."

"You're not fooling me. Something else is going on in those showers. How could you be around a woman that fine and not be tempted to hit it?"

Lincoln joined Tyrone at the card table. For the past month, he no longer required the use of a cane. "Who said I wasn't tempted?" He shifted in his chair. Absently, he started playing with the poker chips. "I mean she's perfect. Not only does she smell good and feel good, mentally she keeps me on my toes. It's amazing really. We're so different—from our childhood to our careers—but yet we're the same. Does that make any sense?"

Tyrone shrugged. "Why are you asking me? I'm divorced. I thought Flex was your relationship adviser."

"Yeah, he thinks I'm secretly dating Henry's sister."

Tyrone shivered as his eyes widened with horror.

"I know." Lincoln took his first swig of beer. "It's a scary thought."

"I don't think his sister has left her house in over a year. Doesn't she have like fifteen cats or something?"

"A few dogs, lizards, and, I believe, a gray parrot. But don't quote me on that."

"And Henry wonders why she has trouble meeting men." Tyrone shook his head. "You know, he tried to get me to go out with her back in college."

"He tried to get everybody to go out with her." Lincoln glanced at his watch. "I wonder why the gang is late."

"They'll be here." Tyrone stretched back and popped a few chips into his mouth. "So how long can you snuggle up to a phone? A brother has needs."

"Tell me about it," Lincoln groaned. This whole abstaining stuff was new to him, too.

"So how long did Flex say it was reasonable to wait?"

"Why? Are you trying to get tips on the side?"

"I'm just curious."

Lincoln shrugged. "He didn't give me a specific date. He just warned me against doing it too soon. I should wait until I'm emotionally invested."

"What a bunch a crap. Men are always emotionally invested. I know I am."

"Yeah, right up until the part where you walk out of the door the next morning."

"Maybe so. But while we're butt naked in the sheets, that woman is my entire world."

"See, that's what I'm talking about. I want her to be my world before and after I sleep with her."

Tyrone groaned.

"You know, this is where I was wrong before," Lincoln continued. "You meet someone and you sleep with them and then you're trying to backpedal and build a relationship. This time I'm going to build the bridge first before I cross it—with Flex's help."

"The man is teaching you what he's learned from his sisters and you're taking that information to win one of the sisters. You don't see anything wrong with that?"

The doorbell rang and Lincoln stood up to answer it.

"Flex said to keep the relationship between A and B. And if it works out, then in the end the brother is only going to care that you're making the sister happy."

"That was when he thought you were talking about Henry's sister."

Lincoln opened his front door and allowed his circus of friends in the house.

"Let's get this party started," Desmond shouted

the moment he crossed the threshold. "I better warn you guys now, I'm feeling mighty lucky tonight."

"Bring it on," Tyrone challenged.

"Hey, where's Flex?" Lincoln asked.

"He's not sure whether he's going to be able to make it," Walter said. "We can go ahead and get started without him."

Desmond chuckled. "Hey, when are you going to tell him that you're tapping his sister's ass, man?"

Lincoln's sharp gaze sliced toward Tyrone.

"Sorry, man. You know I can't keep a lid on something like this."

Heat rushed up Lincoln's body. "I'm not tapping anything, and please tell me none of you idiots have said anything to Flex."

"C'mon," Henry cut in, as he removed his jacket. "Give us a little more credit than that."

"Not to mention, Flex is a big guy," Tyrone said. "He might decide to kill the messenger. If you know what I mean."

A murmur of agreement encircled the table as Lincoln took his seat. "Ty, I can't believe you blabbed."

Desmond's dark features twisted into a frown. "What's the big deal? It's just us. We share everything—unless you're trying to change that too?"

Four sets of eyes narrowed on Lincoln and he was forced to go on the defensive. "It's not like that. It's just that I really like this girl and I'm determined not to make the same mistakes I've made in the past. I'm too old to be hanging out in the clubs or hooking up with the wrong type of women. Women I know going into the relationship are wrong for me. Then I see this exciting firecracker and, man, can she dance!"

"So you actually met her at a club?"

"Actually, the first time I talked to her was on Flex's cell phone."

Tyrone leaned forward at this new piece of news.

"You picked up his sister over his own phone? Have you no shame?"

"No, I didn't pick her up. I wanted to, but Flex sort of cut me off at the knees when I asked about her. So I forgot about it. Then I see her at this club and then the next thing I know she's the hotshot artist rep I went to meet. Don't you see? Fate is playing a hand in all of this."

Tyrone snickered. "I think you need to drink a few beers, do a couple of sit-ups, and stop talking like a girl."

The men laughed as Walter finally started dealing the cards.

"Besides," Tyrone continued, "if Flex is such an expert, then why isn't he married?"

"He just got out of a ten-year relationship before he moved here."

The small group whistled impressively.

"I have a question," Desmond asked, opening a box of cigars and passing them around. "If you're not sleeping with this chick, then what *are* you doing?"

"That's none of your business," Lincoln answered.

"Probably some hot and heavy phone sex," Henry teased, and then elbowed Lincoln. "I ain't playa hating. You got to get it any way you can, right?"

"Change the subject. I'm not going to talk about this."

Desmond lowered his voice to do his impression of Lincoln. "Hey, Peyton, baby. What you got on tonight?"

The table erupted with laughter.

Walter leaned forward. "My thing is, you're not going to be able to hide this from Flex for long," he said. "What are you going to do when she tells her brother the name of her new boyfriend?"

Lincoln drew a breath. "Trust me, that keeps me up at night."

"Why? You two aren't doing anything."

"Still." Lincoln shrugged. "But it'll all be over next Saturday when I go to California for his sister's wedding. I'm supposed to meet the family."

"Sure hope you don't meet Flex's fists," Tyrone scoffed. "It would be a shame for the man who saved your neck to also be the one that takes it."

Lincoln exhaled as he peeked at his cards. "Amen."

It was another day, and another pair of shoes was pinching Peyton's feet when she entered the Peppermill. As usual she was the last sister to make it to the restaurant, and as a result, Michael lit into her.

"Why haven't you picked up your dress yet?"

"I meant to get over there today, I swear, but I was held up at the office." She glanced over at Sheldon, who was busy fanning herself and her big belly. "Are you all right?"

"It's just so damn hot in here," Sheldon complained.

It was actually a bit chilly.

Frankie chuckled. "I think you're going to have that baby tonight."

Michael's face instantly soured. "She better not have that baby until after my wedding."

The girls laughed at the ridiculous demand.

"You're getting a little too controlling," Peyton warned. When their waiter passed the table she ordered a Long Island iced tea. Maybe it would be just the thing to relax her.

"So how are you, P.J.?" Frankie asked, leaning forward.

"Busy as always."

"Huh-uh. You know I passed Cosabellas the other day . . ."

Peyton stiffened.

". . . and I saw you in there buying lingerie."

All eyes swiveled in Peyton's direction. Mentally, she counted to three, and on cue her sisters lobbed questions at her.

"Who is he?" Sheldon asked.

"When did you meet him?" came from Frankie.

"Is it serious?" Michael tossed in.

And at last from Joey, "Is it who I think it is?"

Normally, Peyton would've been annoyed by her sisters' questions, but all thoughts of Lincoln brought a smile to her lips.

"Good heavens, she's blushing," Michael marveled.

Sheldon covered a hand across her heart. "You've been holding out on us? That's blasphemy!"

"It is not." Peyton swatted Sheldon's arm. "And since when is it a crime for a woman to shop for lingerie?" That comment went over like bandits, judging by the number of neck swivels and eye rolls. "Okay, I met this guy in New York."

"I knew it," Joey clapped her hands. "You're still talking to that Lincoln guy, aren't you?"

"Lincoln?" Frankie frowned. "What kind of name is that?"

"I like it," Peyton defended. "I think it's different and sexy."

Sheldon leaned back. "Hmmph. Any bets on how long this will last?"

"I'll give it two weeks," Michael piped in. "By then she'll have a list as long as my arm on what's wrong with him."

"I don't think so," Joey said. "It's already been *three* months."

Peyton settled back in her chair and crossed her arms. "Do you girls mind not betting on me like I'm some kind of racehorse? Just be happy I've found someone I care a lot about." She shrugged. "He seems to really have his act together. He's a strong man who loves working with his hands."

"Uh-huh." Sheldon sipped her Coke. "I want to know if he's been working those strong hands on you."

Frankie, Michael, and Joey leaned in close to hear Peyton's answer.

"As a matter of fact, he's been the perfect gentleman," Peyton boasted.

Everyone's expression deflated and a chorus of "you poor thing" and "heaven forbid" echoed around her before they started laughing.

Peyton joined in. "I know, I know. Gentlemen aren't normally my type."

"I think 'boring' was the word you once used," Michael said. "And frankly, I agree. The worst thing in the world is to fall for a guy who's lousy in bed. I don't care what anyone says, sex is important."

"Damn right." Sheldon patted her pregnant belly for emphasis. "But without a ring, you make sure you wrap it up."

Peyton held up her hands. "I already know all of this. And to be honest, I wasn't the one holding out. I've been giving signals all over the place and nothing happened. Now I'm sort of glad it hasn't. There is such a thing as too much too fast." She smiled to herself while her thoughts drifted to Lincoln. Their long talks every night caused a delicious blush to creep up her cheeks.

"He didn't even try?" Joey asked, frowning. "That's unusual."

"Maybe he needs a little help," Frankie teased.

"Oh, I know a good doctor where he could get those Viagra pills," Sheldon said excitedly.

Everyone stared at her.

"What? You stick to what works."

"I don't think that's going to be the case," Peyton said, finishing her drink.

"Well, it's been three months. Are you guys at least having phone sex?"

Peyton's mouth slackened momentarily and then she remembered whom she was dealing with. "I'll never tell."

"More blasphemy," Michael said. "All I can say is if you've been talking for three months and he hasn't so much as hinted that he wants to sleep with you, then maybe he's gay."

"What?" Peyton waved off the comment. "He's not gay."

"You'd be surprised how many men swing both ways. Go get any E. Lynn Harris book. Girl, those things will open your eyes."

"Oh, Lord," Frankie said, rolling her eyes. "She's gone crazy."

Joey spoke up. "I, for one, am happy for you. Three months have passed and you haven't jumped on a soapbox about what you hate about this guy. Good for you."

"That's because I haven't found anything I hate about him. He's . . . perfect."

"A perfect man?" Frankie chuckled. "Isn't that an oxymoron?"

"Sounds like one to me," Michael agreed.

"He's perfect for me," Peyton amended with a wink.

"So when do we get to meet this perfect man?" Michael inquired.

"Next week." Peyton jiggled her brows. "He's my date for the wedding."

"That explains the lingerie." Sheldon snickered. "Sounds like someone is finally going to try out the goods."

"Ooh," the girls sang.

Her sisters had hit the nail on the head and Peyton was sure her face was as bright as a red rose. Bottom line: she was ready to take the next step. She'd loved their time together and she loved that he was her first and last call of the day. She wanted to move past dreaming about sex with Lincoln to actually experiencing it. And this time, she'd get her way even if she had to chain him to the bedposts.

"Well," Peyton said, while signaling their waiter for a refill, "all I know is no *straight* man will be able to resist me in my new Cosabellas."

Sheldon lifted her glass. "Here's to P.J. and Lincoln getting their groove on."

Everyone lifted their glasses with a chorus of, "Hear! Hear!"

The day before Lincoln left for his trip to California, he stood in the center of Local 1492 Dekalb Fire Department. His old colleagues surrounded him and sang "For He's a Jolly Good Fellow" at full volume. A current of conflicting emotions coursed through his body and clogged in his throat.

Omar Preston walked through the crowd, carrying a large fire truck sheet cake covered in candles. Above the top were the words *We'll miss you*.

Even though he knew this was going to be a difficult thing to get through, it took everything he had to suppress the water works.

The song ended only to be replaced by a thunderous round of applause. Lincoln made a feeble attempt to blow out the candles and received another whoop of cheers.

Chief Zahn appeared suddenly at his side and pounded his back. "The department sure isn't going to be the same around here, Lieutenant Carver."

"I'm not going to be too far away," he assured him. "I've decided to take the fire investigator job with the city."

"Then we're glad to still have you as part of the team."

"Thank you, sir." From the corner of his eye, Lincoln caught a glimpse of Flex conversing with the captain. He excused himself from Zahn once the two men parted company.

"Hey, buddy. You have a minute?" Lincoln asked.

Flex turned and pumped Lincoln's hand. "What do you know? It's the man of the hour."

Lincoln laughed, but inwardly he wasn't at all confident in what he was about to do. "I need to talk with you."

"Sure, what can I do for you?" Flex folded his meaty arms and met Lincoln's gaze.

Lincoln looked around and was uncomfortable with the fact that they were in earshot of so many people. "If we could just go where there's a little more privacy."

Flex frowned. "Is something wrong?"

"No, no. It's nothing like that." His awkward laugh cracked, forcing him to clear his throat. "Maybe we can just go into the captain's office for a sec."

Still frowning, Flex narrowed his eyes to scrutinize him, and then finally he nodded. "All right. Sure."

As Lincoln led the way, he received a few more pats on the back and one good pounding by Omar that nearly caused him to cough up a lung.

"We're going to miss you, Lieutenant," someone shouted.

Lincoln waved to them and stepped into the captain's office. He waited until Flex cleared the threshold before he closed the door.

"Now that you've piqued my curiosity, what can I do for you?"

One look into Flex's intense expression, and

Lincoln's mind was wiped clean of the speech he'd memorized this morning. "It's, uh, about this girl I've been seeing."

"Oh, this is about relationships again?" Flex relaxed and lowered his tall frame into one of the vacant chairs. "Shoot."

"Yeah, well, it's like I said, it's about this girl I've been seeing."

"You mean Henry's sister?"

Lincoln opened his mouth to say no, but there must have been a short somewhere in his brain because the word that stumbled out was "Yes."

"Okay. So what's up? Has something happened?"

Just tell him. "The problem is I'm feeling a little guilty for sneaking behind my friend's back. I know you said to just keep this between A and B, but I feel like I'm being dishonest. The last thing I want to do is ruin my friendship with . . . Henry."

Flex shrugged. "Then just tell him."

"Right." Lincoln nodded, but his burden hadn't lifted. "What would you do?"

Flex's frown returned. "What do you mean?"

Lincoln walked over and took a seat behind the captain's desk. "If a friend of yours just popped up and said that he's been dating one of your sisters behind your back?"

"Probably kill him." Flex shrugged and then laughed.

Lincoln laughed awkwardly along with him.

"Besides, I already had a bad experience once in that arena," Flex added.

"Oh? What happened?" Lincoln asked, but knew the answer.

"Peyton married him. *Big mistake.*" Flex crossed his arms. "He broke her heart—more so than she's willing to admit. There's not a day I don't wish I could open a can of whoop ass on him. So maybe I'm the wrong guy to be asking."

"But you said—"

"See, this is why I said keep it between A and B. That way you can avoid a whole bunch of drama."

Lincoln shook his head. He didn't like any of this. "No. I can't continue to sneak around, like some kind of criminal."

Flex shrugged. "I guess there's one other option."

"What is it?"

"Both of you could sit down with Henry together. That way he'll more likely be influenced by the sister than the back-stabbing friend."

"Hey!"

"Sorry." He chuckled. "C'mon. It's not all gloom and doom. Henry doesn't look like the type to go on a rampage. He's probably going to be fine with it."

Lincoln nodded and made his decision. "You're right. I'll wait until we can both sit down with . . . Henry so we can get his approval."

"Well, there you go." Flex stood up. "I'm so glad that I was able to help."

Lincoln beamed a bright smile at his friend. "I'm glad we had this talk."

"Any time." Flex winked. "Any time."

Chapter 18

"I miss you," Lincoln confessed the moment Peyton answered her phone. He climbed into bed wearing just a pair of black silk boxers.

"We'll see each other soon," her honey-coated voice reminded him. "And I have a surprise for you, too."

"Hmm. A good surprise, I hope." He hit his night switch and folded his free hand behind his head.

"I think so."

Lincoln's imagination took flight as his already broad smile slid wider. "How about giving me a hint?"

"All right." Her voice lightened to a lyrical melody that he'd come to love. "It's strictly for the bedroom."

"Really?" He instantly pictured her in a soft pink teddy fringed in lace and a thong back. "Is this a visual treat?"

"You can say that."

"Is this something you wear?"

"Not for long, I hope."

Lincoln developed an instant hard-on. "You sure know how to torture a guy."

"I'm only trying to give you something to look forward to. I know I'm looking forward to taking this relationship to the next level."

"The next level." He grinned. "Are you sure you're ready for that?" Her slight pause surprised and scared him.

"Maybe I should be asking you that question," she said softly. "Every time I hint at us, uh, getting together, you seem to take a step back. Is there something you're not telling me?"

"No, no. Of course not. Believe me, I want to be with you—more than anything. I also want to make sure that the timing is right. It's important that we know what's between us is more than a physical thing, you know?"

"You sure don't talk like any man I've ever known."

"Maybe that's why you're so crazy about me," he teased. "That—and you're dying to get into my pants."

"Am not!"

"You know you're trying to turn me into your own personal boy toy. Your bedroom is probably filled with a bunch of whips and chains."

"That's not true," she said indignantly, but then burst into laughter.

"I can see you as one of those dominatrix chicks." His image of Peyton in soft pink transformed. Now her shapely body was covered in black liquid latex.

She laughed. "Guess again."

Lincoln wiped the vision from his mind. "Good, I'd hate to tell you that I don't swing that way."

"Ditto. Although you might look cute chained to the bed."

"Not going to happen," Lincoln warned sternly, but continued holding on to a light smile. "So tell me more about this surprise. "Is it itsy-bitsy?"

"Very," she whispered.

Lincoln closed his eyes. "Two-piece or a one-piece?"

"Well, there are several. But what I've picked out for our first night is a two-piece."

Lincoln's solid erection began to throb. "Describe it to me."

Peyton painted an image of her dressed in a two-piece baby-blue bra and thong set on the canvas in his mind. She twirled around in high-heel pumps and gave him an eyeful of her bare apple-shaped booty.

"Absolutely gorgeous," he whispered into the phone.

"Can you picture it?" she asked.

"Oh yes." The Peyton in his head walked toward him in small measured steps. As he gazed into her eyes, he saw the warm glint of desire.

Lincoln leaned back against the room's king-size bed and watched his fantasy seductress climb aboard and inch toward him. She didn't stop until she crawled up the length of his body and sat straddled across his hips. From this angle, he took pleasure in admiring her hard abs and ample breasts. So much so he couldn't stop himself from sliding his hands up her soft skin and cupping her firm breasts.

Peyton, too, could see the created fantasy in her head. She could almost feel the way he gently squeezed her breasts. Her insides fluttered with excitement. She leaned forward and brushed her lips against his and was completely unprepared for how an array of emotions blended and snaked through her like a living thing.

His hands deserted her breasts and glided to her back where they busily unhooked the bra. In no time the bra was sent flying across the bed and his large hands reclaimed their position around her sensitive mounds.

Their kiss deepened. The taste of him was frighteningly real and earth-shatteringly delicious, but it wasn't long before their mouths grew hungry and downright possessive.

"Then I'll roll you onto your back." Lincoln's ragged voice drifted over the phone. "And place small kisses down the side of your neck."

Peyton quivered and slid her hands into his short-cropped hair. It seemed to take forever for his mouth to settle around one of her tanned nipples, and when he did she whimpered. His hands, however, continued their journey downward. She lifted her hips to help him remove that brand-new thong.

As she imagined his fingers dipping inside her, a soft moan fell from her lips and filled the phone line.

Lincoln's heart hammered. The very idea of her warm slick passage was enough to drive him over the edge. She was squirming beneath him while her body rocked to a rhythm he'd set. "Are you ready for me?"

"Yes." Her voice quivered over the line. Her breathing became nothing more than thin vapors. How was it possible to be shivering when her body was burning up? It didn't make sense.

Lincoln's hands explored her body with light intrusive strokes, while his soft full lips rained kisses along her breasts, stomach, and thighs.

"I want you," he whispered. "I need you."

The declaration brought a sheen of tears to moisten her eyes as she quivered beneath his exploration. He described how his head lowered and Peyton could actually feel the slight brush against the triangle of curls nestled between her legs.

Her hands touched where his mouth laved in their shared fantasy. He deepened the intimate kiss, reveling in her rich, hot flavor. Peyton's nail raked his skin and, in no time, her husky cries filled the room and the line linking them together.

"Come for me," Lincoln instructed.

"Yes." Peyton increased her rhythm until she was shuddering and writing against the bed. Suddenly everything began to tingle while air escaped her lungs in short puffs.

Lincoln reveled in the sound that was taking place over the phone. So much so, his hand lowered to stroke his throbbing flesh. "I can't wait any longer. I need to be inside you."

In the fantasy, Lincoln pushed himself up onto his knees and crawled up the length of her body. She reached and pulled him close, locking her legs around his hips. He found her mouth and shared her taste. An erotic kiss that only fed his pleasure.

Slowly, he eased inside her silken walls and nearly cried out at how her soft, warm passage closed tight around him. A perfect fit—a perfect match.

Gently, he rocked inside her, feeling that he'd at last found heaven. Her hips matched his tempo and both were in for an exquisite ride. His name fell effortlessly from her lips and soon became a chanted mantra she could not stop repeating.

Greedy for more, she increased their pacing until their skin was dewed with sweat. The contest became who could outlast the other, but Peyton could already feel herself weakening. There was no denying that something was beginning to blossom inside her.

Lincoln's heavy breathing transformed into guttural groans while her name, as well as a few biblical ones, burst from him.

Regardless, Peyton was the first to cry out at her body's explosion. But Lincoln wasn't too far behind and their voices blended in a glorious harmony.

For a while afterward, the couple laughed at

themselves and simultaneously tried to catch their breath.

"That was intense," she said, and then emitted a small yawn.

"I know I'm good when I can put you to sleep." He chuckled, and surprised himself when he, too, yawned.

"Ditto." She laughed. "Of course, you know that just qualified for round one in my book. If you were really here, that would have just been an appetizer."

"What is this, sexual trash talk?"

"Hey, I'm just warning you," she said. "I'm a woman who goes after what she wants."

"All right. Don't start anything you can't back up. When I get there I don't want to hear 'I'm too tired' or 'I have a headache.' "

"Uh-huh. And I don't want to hear 'Oh, my ankle is killing me' or 'my painkillers made me sleepy,' " she equally challenged.

"Okay, that's low," he chuckled. "You're making fun of an injured man."

"There's no disabled list in this ball game," she warned.

"You have yourself a deal." He climbed out of bed and headed toward the shower. It was time for them to take that next step, he told himself. Mainly because there was no doubt that he was emotionally invested in Peyton Garner. In the past month, he had thought of little else. Their weekend excursions were nice, but way too short.

The most important thing was, he understood her. Hot damn. For the first time in his life, he understood what motivated a woman, what made her happy, and what she expected out of him. And honesty was one of those things.

"Peyton, when I get out there . . . we have to talk."

There was a slight pause over the line.

"Is something wrong?" she inquired in a voice filled with suspicion.

"No, no. Nothing like that. It's just that what I have to tell you, I have to do it in person."

Silence.

"P.J.?"

"Yeah, I guess, but I have to admit you have me curious."

"I'm curious to see those outfits. So we both have something to look forward to."

She laughed. "All right. I'll let it go. Your flight lands at two tomorrow, right?"

"You got it. Flight 801."

"Then I'll meet you at baggage claim."

"It's a date. Love you, bye." It wasn't until the line buzzed with silence that Lincoln realized what he'd said, but before he could try to save face, her soft reply filtered over the line.

"I love you, too."

Chapter 19

Lincoln woke up on time, had his bags packed and ready, but the snag in his schedule came when Tyrone was forty minutes late in picking him up from the airport.

"Sorry, man. Traffic is crazy." Tyrone grabbed a few of his bags and headed out. "Radio said something about a tractor trailer being turned over on I-285. We're going to have to take an alternate route."

"We're not going to miss my flight, are we?"

"Not with Superman at the helm," he assured him. "I'll get you there with time to spare." Tyrone opened the back of his Explorer and crammed in the luggage.

Uncomforted, Lincoln glanced at his watch. "I have a bad feeling about this."

Peyton woke up early. Her body was positively humming from her heady experience with Lincoln last night. If he was that good during phone sex, what would the real thing be like?

Stretching out of bed with a glowing smile, she

headed toward the bathroom for her morning shower. Even then she was unable to get him out of her mind.

Am I in love?

As she stood still beneath the pounding shower, she considered the notion. *I can't be.*

Granted, what she felt for Lincoln was deeper than anything she had experienced before, but she was still frightened by the idea of giving up complete control.

No. This was nothing more than having a good time.

New York was great, Savannah was wonderful, and Las Vegas was the most romantic trip she'd ever taken. The most amazing thing was that she'd been to all those places before. However, being there with Lincoln was like experiencing everything for the first time.

She stepped out of the shower more confused than ever. She wanted to make love to Lincoln, but she wasn't ready to fall in love.

However, the words she'd spoken last night haunted her. "I love you," she quoted herself. Why in the hell did she say that?

Peyton turned off the water in time to hear the doorbell. Rushing out of the bathroom, she grabbed her satin robe and cringed at how much it stuck to her body.

The doorbell rang again and she nearly tripped over the vacuum cleaner she'd left in the hallway. "I'm coming," she shouted. A minute later, she reached the door and was surprised to see Frankie.

"Good. You're up," she said, stepping into the house. "We've been drafted to pick up Flex from the airport."

Peyton closed the door behind her sister. "Whoa. Whoa. I thought Flex was coming tomorrow."

"Sheldon got the dates wrong. She blames it on her hormones being out of whack." Frankie rolled her eyes, and then continued on to the kitchen. "You haven't made any coffee yet?"

"I was in the shower," Peyton said, following her. "What time is he supposed to land?"

"Three o'clock in San Francisco."

"I can't. You're going to have to get Joey or Michael to go with you. I have plans."

Frankie's eyebrows dipped together. "What do you mean? We haven't seen Flex in a year. Can't you put off whatever it is?"

"Lincoln is coming into town today. Two o'clock at the San Jose Airport." Peyton leaned against the refrigerator. "I have *a lot* planned."

Frankie's lips twitched upward. "Ah, tonight is the night, huh?"

"You can say that."

"Since when is getting laid more important than family?" Frankie asked sweetly.

"Don't give me that. Flex is not being abandoned. There are plenty of other family members. Take Daddy. That will be a good way to force those two to start talking again."

Frankie held up a finger and started to protest, and then she stopped to think about it. "You know, that's a good idea."

"Of course it is. I thought of it, didn't I?" She winked. "I have to finish getting ready, I want to stop by the gym and get in a workout—or should I say 'a warm-up' in?—before Lincoln arrives."

"You go, girl."

Lincoln missed his flight.

"I don't believe this." He sank his head into his

hands for a brief moment while he stood at the ticket counter. "When is your next flight to San Jose?"

"Let me just check on that for you," the male ticket agent said, and then began typing away. After inputting enough keystrokes for a great American novel, he looked up at him. "It looks like we have a spot on the ten-fifteen."

"P.M.?"

The agent checked again. "Yes, sir."

Lincoln's head fell back into his hands with a groan.

The typing continued in front of him. "But if you're willing to fly into San Francisco, I can get you on the one o'clock flight. It leaves in twenty minutes."

"It's a deal." Lincoln dug into his back pocket for his wallet. Maybe the day wasn't doomed after all.

On his way to his terminal, he called Peyton at home and was disappointed when he reached her answering machine.

"Hey, baby. Linc here. There's been a slight change in plans." He quickly left his new flight information and then hoped for the best.

Minutes later, he was settled into a nice window seat when he looked up and was stunned to see someone familiar boarding the plane.

Flex!

Immediately, Lincoln shot out a hand to grab one of the airline's catalogs and buried his face behind its pages. *What if his seat is in my row?* The very thought made him ill.

He waited a few minutes while his stomach twisted into knots before he chanced a peek around the catalog. Just two rows ahead of him, Flex Adams sat in a window seat. *When it rains, it pours.*

Lincoln lowered his catalog and took another look at his watch. Would he be able to avoid Flex's attention during the five-hour flight? *Lord, I hope so.*

* * *

Flex was a basket case.

Armed with a new story about his recent breakup with Trey, he swore that he would never lie to his family again. It was just too exhausting and too high a price to pay to save face with Morgan. Of course, this story would undoubtedly compel them to throw the much-dreaded pity party. However, after a few days or months, it would all be over.

Once the plane had finally taken off and he was permitted to remove his seat belt, Flex couldn't remain in his seat. Every few minutes, it seemed, he had to go the restroom. It didn't take long for his frequent trips to annoy the rest of the people in his row. After two hours, the man on the end offered to exchange seats with him.

In review, he attributed his problem to nerves. Flex had never been a fan of flying. On one trip to the restroom, he noticed one guy who kept a magazine draped over his face while he slept. Maybe that was what he needed to do: sleep through the rest of the flight.

This time when Flex returned to his chair, he bought a headset, selected a classical music station, and forced himself to sleep.

Lincoln swore that if Flex stood up one more time, he was just going to put his buddy out of his misery. *The man has to have a urinary tract infection or something.*

Rolling his eyes, Lincoln focused on his new problem. If Peyton was at his gate when . . . no, she wouldn't be allowed at the gate, she would meet him at baggage claim. But if Flex was going to the same terminal, wouldn't she spot her brother as well? Flex was a tall man—not easily missed.

Around and around Lincoln's thoughts chased each other. He had no ready solution, other than to pray; and judging by his day so far, no miracles were in sight.

When the plane was at last preparing for landing, Lincoln was mentally exhausted. Though he would rather talk to Peyton first, if today were going to be the day he confronted Flex about their relationship, then so be it.

Flex woke up just as the fasten-seat-belt light switched on. This was the part he hated: landing. He tensed in his seat as the plane descended and he fought back another incredible urge to run to the restroom. However, touchdown wasn't as bad as he feared, and before he knew it they were rolling toward their gate.

On cue, everyone stood and started removing their things from the overhead compartments. He followed the line out off the plane, feeling good to be back in sunny California. As he followed the airport's signs, directing him to baggage claim, the excitement of seeing his family took root.

Lincoln stayed several feet behind Flex. The hope of getting out of this sticky situation was dim. At baggage claim, Lincoln lingered in the background.

"Susie, come back here," a female screeched.

Lincoln turned just as a runaway child bolted by him.

The mother, however, remained hot on the little girl's trail.

It was a small ruckus, but it was big enough to cause Flex to turn around.

"Lincoln?"

"Flex!" Lincoln exclaimed and forced a look of surprise. "How's it going, buddy?" He reached his friend's side and slapped his back in greeting.

Flex's expression twisted in confusion. "What are you doing here?" he asked, glancing around. "Were we on the same flight?"

"Francis!" a male voice boomed toward them.

Flex's expression fell seconds before an older mirror image of himself appeared at his side and pulled him into a rough embrace. "Dad?"

Lincoln's eyebrows rose at the man's identity. *Peyton's father.* Together the two men looked like a large section of a brick wall. Tall, broad-shouldered, and more than a little intimidating.

"What, you're not happy to see your old man?"

Flex blinked. "No. It's nothing like that . . . I'm just . . . surprised."

"Is that my handsome baby brother?"

Lincoln watched a taller, thicker version of Peyton wrap her arms around Flex. The love she had for her brother radiated in her smile.

Suddenly, she noticed Lincoln. "Oh, where are our manners?" She pulled out of Flex's arms to approach him.

"Uh, Frankie. Wait a minute," Flex said, reaching for her arm.

"Just a sec, Flex. I don't want your friend to think we're being rude."

Their father also approached.

"Hi," she said, thrusting out her hand. "I'm Franklin Becker, this is our father, Marlin Adams, and you must be Trey?"

Lincoln blinked. "Yes, ma'am. As a matter of fact, I am."

Chapter 20

"Welcome to the family." Marlin's strong arms pulled Lincoln into a tight bear hug.

Unsure of what to make of this sudden turn of events, he cast a look over at Flex and was surprised to see his friend's face lose much of its coloring. He tried to wait until Marlin released him, but the hug held on longer than was necessary.

"Uh, sir, it's, uh, nice to meet you."

Marlin finally released his death grip and stepped back, but to Lincoln's surprise the man seemed to have tears in his eyes.

"This is a happy day for me," Marlin said, wiping at the stray tear that had escaped. "I swore this time, I was going to be here for my boy. But I have to warn you, I'm kind of new to this sort of thing."

"Dad." Flex jumped to stand next to Lincoln. "We can talk about all of this once we get back to the house."

"Talk about what?" Lincoln glanced at his friend.

"Flex is right," Frankie cut in. "Let's just grab your luggage and head back to the house." She draped an arm around Lincoln. "Everyone is just dying to meet you, Trey."

Lincoln's eyebrows rose. "You guys already know about us?"

Frankie released a girlish giggle that was nearly as adorable as Peyton's. "Of course we know. Nothing stays a secret in this family. You better get used to that."

"What a relief." He relaxed. "I can't tell you how nervous I was about this whole thing." Lincoln glanced over at his buddy, wearing a wide smile. How long had Flex known about him and his sister?

"Oh, isn't this great, Daddy?" She placed her hands against her face and then pulled Lincoln into her embrace. "I like you already."

When he was finally released, Lincoln puffed out his chest. "I'm happy to hear that. I like you, too." He glanced around. "Where is Peyton?"

"Oh, she couldn't make it. But she's promised to swing by Dad's a little later."

Lincoln nodded, still unable to believe this turn of events. As everyone moved toward the conveyor belt spinning everyone's luggage, Lincoln nudged Flex in the side. "I owe you one, dog," he whispered. "You had me sweating bullets all this time."

"What in the hell are you talking about?" Flex hissed back. "Why are you here?"

Lincoln frowned. "What do you mean, why?"

"Hey, Flex, is this one yours?" Frankie asked, grabbing a bag.

"Yep," Marlin answered for his son. "That's one of the pieces I gave him before he left."

Flex returned his attention and his angry face to Lincoln. "I mean, why? What's going on?"

Scratching his head, Lincoln tried to discern whether he'd been cast in an episode of the *Twilight*

Zone. "I'm here for the same reason you are," he answered.

"I highly doubt it. I'm here for my sister's wedding."

"I know. So am I."

"Why in the hell would you—"

"How about this one, Flex?" Frankie asked.

"Check the name tag," he said, without casting a glance in their direction.

"Peyton invited me," Lincoln said. "Didn't you guys just say that you knew about us?"

Flex's face lost even more color. "You . . . and Peyton?"

"I thought you knew?"

"How in the hell would I know?" he barked.

Lincoln jerked in reaction and then glanced around.

Marlin approached. "Is everything okay with you two?"

Flex's scowl was quickly replaced by a shellacked grin. "Never better," he assured his father. "We're just having a private discussion."

"Well, that's going to have to wait. Sheldon and Michael have us on a tight schedule. They're cooking dinner for you boys, and you know how they can get when things don't go according to plan." Marlin winked at Lincoln. "You'll find out soon enough if we don't hurry."

"You got it," Lincoln said, and moved to search for his bags.

A few minutes later, everyone had their things and headed out of the airport. It was Lincoln's first time out to the West Coast and when he stepped out into the blaze of the July sunshine, he could already see why so many people flocked to the state of nirvana.

While Lincoln followed Frankie and Marlin to an impressive silver Lexus LX, he couldn't help but wonder why the two seemed to know why he was there and Flex didn't. Had Peyton figured everything out, but hadn't told her brother? But then why had he initially pretended to be in the loop?

After all the bags were packed, Lincoln and Flex climbed into the backseats and waited until their escorts climbed in as well.

"Linc, I don't know what's going on, but you have to play along with this until we reach my father's house."

"Play along with what?"

Flex closed his eyes and wrung his hands. "Please. I'll explain everything once we get to the house. I swear."

Lincoln had never seen him like this. "All right. Hey, we're dogs, right?"

"Thanks." Flex heaved a heavy sigh, but he didn't look too relieved.

"Is everybody ready?" Marlin asked, taking his place behind the steering wheel.

Frankie lowered herself into her seat and strapped on her seat belt.

"Ready when you are," Lincoln announced.

She turned in her seat and flashed him another smile. "We have a guest room all prepared for you," she said. "We want to make your stay as comfortable as possible."

"I'm going to be staying at your father's house?" Lincoln swallowed. Was he being set up for an ambush interrogation? Did the older man always come off as a sweet, affectionate guy in the beginning only to become a CIA operative when no one was looking?

"I hope you don't mind, Flex. But I think you and Daddy probably need some time alone."

"I think we'll just stay at a hotel or something," Flex said. There was no mistaking the hint of annoyance laced in his voice.

When Marlin's eyes lifted to the rearview mirror to stare back at his son, Lincoln saw the hurt in the elder's gaze.

Frankie cleared her throat. "There's no reason to be like this, Flex. This is a time for celebration and we should all work to make bygones be bygones."

Flex huffed out a breath, but he still refused to look at his father. "You know how much I hate it when you guys do things without checking with me first."

"Then let me ask you now," Marlin said. "Do you want to stay with me?"

Still Flex didn't look up and he didn't answer either.

"Of course we will," Lincoln said. "We would be happy to." Apparently it was the wrong answer, judging by the glare Flex shifted in his direction.

Lincoln leaned over to whisper, "What's the matter with you? This is your father."

"Good." Frankie clasped her hands together. "It's settled. Trey, I can already tell why you two—"

"Frankie, can't we talk about something else?" Flex said, tersely.

"What? I was just going to say—"

"Please?"

"All right, all right." She shrugged, and then turned back into her seat. "I can take a hint."

Lincoln frowned during the layering tension. At the airport everyone was happy-go-lucky and now it seemed some invisible lines had been drawn.

Marlin cleared his throat and cast a glance over his shoulder at Lincoln. "So tell us a little about yourself, Trey. Flex hasn't told us too much about you."

Lincoln cleared his throat. "Well, there's not much to tell. I'm a retired firefighter—"

"I say there's no greater profession. Don't you agree, Francis?" Marlin's face blossomed into a smile.

"Dad, please call me Flex." Flex rubbed at his temples.

"Yeah, sure. I forgot." Marlin's smile cracked.

Lincoln popped his friend on the shoulder and hissed, "Get a grip." He didn't care if he was being out of line. Where he grew up, a child always talked to parents or any elders with respect. The way he saw it, Flex's behavior was just plain inexcusable.

"I agree with you, Mr. Adams," Lincoln said. "I'll miss being with the department, but I'm hoping that becoming an inspector will fill me with the same sense of accomplishment."

Marlin's smile returned to its previous brilliance. "You know, I've been in the game for nearly forty years."

"Yes, I heard you had quite an impressive career."

"Well, I'm glad my son hasn't just told you the bad things about me."

Lincoln frowned. "Well, both Flex and Peyton have told me quite a bit."

"Peyton?" Flex whispered.

Lincoln met his friend's stare and shrugged. "Yeah, she talks of little else."

In an instant, Flex's strong hand clamped onto his arm. Lincoln even spotted a lightning bolt flash in Flex's eyes.

Frankie laughed. "Don't tell me that Peyton's been talking to Trey behind your back, Flex."

Now Lincoln was really confused.

"Apparently," Flex seethed.

"Don't get too angry, Fran . . . Flex. I'm sure she was just looking out for you. You know how your sisters are. They mean well."

Lincoln scratched his head. It was clear now that Flex didn't know about him and Peyton, and most assuredly he would pay for that later; but if Frankie and

Marlin also didn't know about them, then what the hell was going on?

"Play along," Flex warned, with a note of desperation, and then released his hold on Lincoln's arm.

How could he play when he didn't even know the name of the game?

For the rest of the ride, the conversation was kept to a minimum after Flex kept cutting people off or changing the subject. By the time they arrived at the Adams family home, Lincoln didn't know what to make of anything. Not to mention, he wasn't in the door for more than a few seconds before two more women wrenched him into their embrace.

"Oh, look at you. You sure are a cutie—and tall."

Lincoln instantly liked her. "You must be Sheldon," he guessed. "Mind if I feel if junior is kicking today?"

Sheldon took his hand and placed it on her belly.

"What the heck is he doing in there?" he asked. "Feels like he's doing a few layups."

"My bladder and I are well aware of that," she said, and then wobbled away to find a chair.

"Hi. I'm Michael. I'd say cute is an understatement," she said, grinning up at him. "They always say that the good ones are either taken or gay." She tweaked his cheek.

"In a couple of days, you'll be off the market, too," Lincoln reminded her.

She blushed. "Trust me. It's been a long time coming." She turned toward her brother. "I'm glad you kept your word. I was expecting some kind of excuse."

Flex smiled, but didn't meet her gaze. "Where's Joey?" he asked.

"L.A. She's attending some screenwriters conference. She'll be back later tonight."

"No husbands?"

"Working. Though my Phil promised to swing by in time for dinner."

"So where do our bags go?" Lincoln asked.

"Oh, I'll show you." Michael turned toward the stairs.

"That's okay, I'll show him where the guest room is," Flex said.

"Now, let me do my job as hostess," Michael said, and then took Lincoln by the hand. "You two follow me."

Lincoln followed. It was a nice two-story brick house with all the comforts of home.

"Here we are," Michael announced. "You two will be staying in here."

Lincoln entered the room and then glanced around. "There's only one bed."

"I know," Michael said, reaching over to pat Flex on the arm. "It wasn't easy to convince Dad to put a king-size bed in here." She turned back to Lincoln. "Now you guys get settled. Sheldon can't stay long, so we're having an early dinner. We're having Flex's favorite dish." She tweaked Lincoln's cheeks again. "You're sure a cutie."

Lincoln watched her as she left the room and then his eyes traveled back to the king-size bed.

Flex closed the door.

"I think you need to start talking," Lincoln said, trying to keep his panic to just a mild heart attack.

Flex shifted his weight nervously. "Maybe you should sit down."

The only place to sit was the bed. "I'd rather stand."

"Okay, um. My family, uh, are under the impression that, uh . . . that you and I are . . . a couple."

Chapter 21

Lincoln stared at him.

Flex held up his hands and tried to diffuse the situation. "I know you're upset, but—"

"They think that I'm—"

"I shouldn't have lied to them, but—"

"They think that we're—"

"I never dreamed they'd ever meet you. I just wanted them to think I was over Morgan."

"Morgan . . . is a guy?"

"I know this is coming as a complete shock, but what are the chances of something like this happening? I mean, I just picked your name off the top of my head. I don't think of you in that way. No offense."

"None taken."

"This mess, which by the way could've been avoided if you'd told me you were dating my sister—"

"This is *my* fault?" Lincoln thundered. "I was just following your lousy advice."

"My advice?"

"Yeah. You said for A and B to sit down with the brother and talk to him about their relationship.

Remember? So, I thought this was the perfect time to do that."

"You're supposed to be dating *Henry's* sister."

"Spoken like a man who's never met Henry's sister."

Flex drew a deep breath. "Okay, there has to be a way that we can get through this."

"Yeah, you can go down there and tell them I'm not gay," Lincoln said in a near shout.

"Will you lower your voice?" Flex hissed. "Do you want everyone to hear you?"

"As a matter of fact, I do." Lincoln paced. "It's not that I have a problem with you being gay. Whatever floats your boat, but there's no way in hell I'm going to let your family keep believing that I'm your boyfriend."

"I can't tell them the truth now."

"Then I'll do it." Lincoln moved toward the door, but was stopped when Flex's iron grip closed around his arm.

"Wait. Do you have any idea what this is going to do to me? Have you ever had five women throw you a pity party? And Michael is never going to forget me lying to her."

"What it's going to do to you? What about me?"

"You can't do me this one favor? I did, after all, save your life."

Lincoln's eyes rounded with incredulity. "I can't believe you brought that up."

"I'm desperate," Flex said. "And I would do it for you."

"Do what for me—pretend to be my boyfriend?" he asked. "You can file that in the 'never going to happen' column. Besides, what are you going to do when Peyton or Joey gets here?"

"You met Joey, too?"

"In New York."

Understanding dawned in Flex's eyes. "The art agent." He smacked his head.

"Look, man," Lincoln said. "I'm sorry about this. I'm truly am, but I can't help you. You have to go down there and tell your family the truth."

Flex continued to shake off the logical solution. "I'll never hear the end of this."

A phone's shrill ring filled the room.

Lincoln pulled out the cell from his pocket. When he read the screen ID, he looked at Flex. "It's Peyton."

Flex rolled his eyes.

"Hey, sweetheart," he answered. "No, I got a ride from the airport. I, uh, didn't think you received my message. Uh, where am I?" He looked up at his buddy.

Flex frantically shook his head and waved his hands.

"Hold on a sec." Lincoln covered the receiver with his hands. "What do you expect for me to tell her? She's at the airport looking for me."

"Tell her you're anywhere but here," Flex hissed. "I need more time to figure this out."

Lincoln's shoulders deflated.

"Please," Flex added. "I'll figure something out."

"This is insane," Lincoln hissed and then brought the phone back to his ear. "I, uh, got a rental car and I'm headed out to your place. Uh-huh. I'm sorry I had you driving all over the state. I promise I'll make it up to you tonight."

Flex winced.

"You want to go to your father's house tonight?" His gaze returned to his friend to see the same frantic shaking and waving. "You have to meet your brother's new *boyfriend?*" He wanted to laugh. "No, no. I don't think that you told me that he was gay."

Lincoln covered the receiver again. "I'm going to *kill* you."

"Uh, baby, do we have to go tonight? Can't we meet this, uh, guy tomorrow? I mean I'm going to be here for a full week after all. Uh-huh. Well, call your sisters and then I'll meet you at your place. How about that? All right, see you then. Bye."

"Thank you, Linc." Flex exhaled. "I owe you one."

Lincoln had to sit down. "Trust me, buddy. You can't begin to pay this back."

All of Peyton's plans had been blown out of the water. Now, how was she going to tell Michael that she wasn't going to be able to come over and show off her new man? Michael was a stickler when it came to schedules.

She waited until she made it back to her car before she dialed her father's number and held her breath. "Hey, Mike. It's me."

"Me who?"

"P.J." She rolled her eyes. "Look, something has come up. Lincoln and I aren't going to be able to come for dinner."

"I'm going to pretend that you didn't say that."

"I'm serious, Mike. We aren't going to make it. Lincoln missed his flight." She closed her eyes and crossed her fingers. "He's coming in later."

A long silence trailed after her lie.

"What time is he landing? Maybe you can come along."

"Can't. I'm already here in San Francisco. I'll never make it there and then come back in time."

Michael exhaled. "I'm already not liking this boyfriend of yours. How the heck did he miss his flight?"

"It doesn't matter. All is not lost. You can meet Lincoln tomorrow. What's the big deal?"

"Well, I wanted you to meet Trey." Michael lowered her voice. "I mean this guy is a real looker. It's the first guy Flex has dated that has gotten me a little hot and bothered myself."

"Hey, hey. You're practically a married woman," Peyton joked.

"I haven't walked down the aisle yet."

Peyton laughed as she started her car. "You're a little disturbed if you're thinking about jumping our brother's boyfriend. Pull yourself together."

"I'm telling you, girl, when you meet Trey you'll probably want to dump this Lincoln character and try to sway this brother onto the straight and narrow."

"There're only two problems with that idea. Number one, he's gay; number two, he's Flex's man."

"Love isn't perfect." Michael chuckled. "But there's another reason why you should come over." She lowered her voice. "I invited Morgan over for dinner."

"What?" Peyton pressed her brakes. "Have you lost your mind?"

"Are you kidding? It's going to be great. What better way for Flex to prove that he's moved on? I'm telling you, Morgan is going to take one look at Trey and just break down."

"Okay. I'm going to say something that I've never said before, and I mean this with love and sincerity: you need help."

Michael laughed. "Trust me. I know what I'm doing."

"I highly doubt that. Isn't Morgan dating someone new?"

"Actually, Sheldon said that she heard through the grapevine—her hairdresser—that Morgan and his sugar daddy broke up a few weeks ago."

"So Morgan thinks he's coming to over to make up with Flex?"

"Something like that."

Peyton couldn't believe what she was hearing.

"Listen to me. You are asking for trouble. It's bad enough that we have Flex staying with Daddy after their ugly fight, and now you're going to surprise Flex by inviting for dinner the very person he moved to get away from? Don't you see this could blow up in your face? What are you going to do if he storms out and refuses to go to the wedding?"

"Don't be silly. He would never do that. Besides, I know what's best for all concerned. Most of all, I know Flex. He'll thank me for giving him the opportunity to give Morgan his comeuppance."

"You're delusional and I don't want any part of this." Peyton eased off the brake and pulled out into traffic. "Tell you what, Lincoln and I will stop by in the morning after the dust settles."

Michael's laughter filtered through the lines. "I'm telling you, girl. Tonight is going to be a night to remember."

Chapter 22

When Lincoln woke up this morning, he never imagined that his day would've turned out this way. Even now, he couldn't believe a missed flight would lead to him pretending to be Flex's boyfriend.

Minutes after talking with Peyton, he called Enterprise and requested a rental car to be delivered to the Adams home.

"Well, that's that," he told Flex. "How far does Peyton live from here?"

"Two doors down." Flex paced the floor. "Sheldon is two doors up, Frankie is around the block, and Michael and her fiancé remodeled the basement."

"You guys have a severe case of separation anxiety," Lincoln said, shaking his head. "Where did you and Morgan live?"

"In Sunnyvale. I couldn't very well have my father—" He stopped and drew a deep breath.

Curious, Lincoln crossed his arms and watched his friend start pacing again. "What's the story between you two, anyway? On the way here, I couldn't have cut the tension in the car with a chain saw."

"It's nothing." Flex waved him off. "By the way, when we get back home—"

"Mum's the word." Lincoln pretended to zip his lips.

Flex's shoulder slumped and he took a spot next to Lincoln on the bed. "There's no way to get out of this. If we faked a fight, then what are we going to say when you're introduced as Peyton's new boyfriend?"

"We can always say you were just a fling." Lincoln laughed.

"Really?"

"Hell no." Lincoln leaned away from him. "What's wrong with you? It's obvious that your family just wants you to be happy. They love you. Any blind man can see that. So you lied." He shrugged. "It's not the end of the world. They'll forgive you."

Flex slumped his head even lower.

"I, on the other hand, will kill you if you don't fix this mess."

"All right, all right."

A knock sounded at the door and Frankie's voice filtered through. "Dinner's ready."

"We'll be right there," Flex called out, and then glanced over at Lincoln. "Regardless, man. Thanks for not completely freaking out on me."

Lincoln nodded, and then gave him a good hearty pat on the back. "You know, I've known the guys in our department for a long time. I can honesty say that you're never going to meet a better group of guys. There's no reason you can't be who you are with them. Remember that."

Finally a small smile hooked the corners of Flex's mouth. "Thanks. I needed to hear that." He took a deep breath and stood. "C'mon. Let's go and clear this thing up."

"Sounds good." Lincoln stood. "Looks like for once I was able to help you through a problem, huh?"

"Yeah, yeah." Flex opened the bedroom door. "Don't let it go to your head though."

Lincoln laughed and glanced at his watch before he followed his friend. "Hey, how much time do you think I have before Peyton gets home?"

"About thirty minutes," Flex whispered back. "And by the way, we still need to discuss this thing about you dating my sister."

"You have to be kidding. I'm good enough for you, but not good enough for your sister?"

Flex's large shoulders vibrated with silent laughter, but midway down the staircase he came to an abrupt halt. "Morgan?"

"Hello, Francis."

Morgan? Lincoln glanced over Flex's shoulder at a well-groomed brother who was unbelievably shorter than Tyrone.

"What are you doing here?" Flex asked.

Morgan suddenly looked uncomfortable. "I was invited."

Flex's head swiveled toward his sisters.

The three of them blinked prettily back up at him.

"There's definitely plenty of lasagna to go around," Sheldon said. She waltzed over to Morgan and reached for his jacket. "Let me take that for you."

Lincoln wasn't exactly sure what was going on, but the dynamics had changed, and there was suddenly enough tension in the room to choke an elephant.

"I take it you weren't told I was coming?" Morgan concluded as he slid out his jacket.

Flex didn't respond, nor did he move.

Marlin suddenly appeared from somewhere in the back. He stopped short when he saw Morgan and then looked toward the stairwell where Flex and Lincoln stood rooted. "I just want to go on record, I have nothing to do with this."

* * *

Peyton sped down Highway 101 with a lead foot.

It wasn't until she was halfway home that she wondered how Lincoln knew how to get to her house, but then dismissed that thought when she realized anything was possible with today's technology.

"Tonight is going to perfect," she repeated to herself. "At least it should be better than running across California for most of the day."

She thought about the last three months, she even smiled when an image of Lincoln's handsome face popped into her mind. "If Michael thinks this Trey is fine, wait until she sees my Lincoln," she mused.

But what was she going to feed him? She hadn't planned on cooking tonight. "Maybe I could just swing by Dad's and steal some lasagna."

Just when she was warming up to that idea, a pair of flashing blue lights caught her attention in the rearview mirror. "Great. What else can go wrong today?"

"Why don't we all just sit down for dinner?" Sheldon said, clapping her hands together.

"I know I'm starved," Morgan said. His smile was a little too wide and his posture a bit stiff as he smiled at everyone.

Lincoln leaned forward to whisper near Flex's ear, "Maybe it's a good idea that we move from off the stairs."

Flex didn't respond, but he did finally descend the rest of the stairs.

"Good," Frankie said, and appeared somewhat relieved that World War III hadn't transpired—yet.

"Uh, you guys go ahead," Lincoln said. "I need to talk to Flex for a minute."

"Oh, certainly." Michael swept everyone out of the

foyer, while beaming her own smile to everyone. "You two don't take too long."

The doorbell rang.

Michael made a one-eighty to answer it.

"I'll get it," Flex seethed. "I think you've done enough for one evening."

She jumped back as if her brother had turned into a rattlesnake. "C'mon. Surely, you're not angry." She actually succeeded in looking astonished. "We did this for you."

The doorbell rang again.

"Maybe I should get it," Lincoln mumbled, and opened the door. At least it wasn't another surprise guest, but the delivery of his rental car.

"What do need a rental car for?" Michael asked, trying to peek around her brother to see who was at the door.

"So we don't have to rely on the family for transportation," Flex told her and then jumped back on her case. "You really have some nerve inviting Morgan here. He's the last person I want to see."

"I, uh, am going to test drive the car," Lincoln said from the doorway. "I'll be right back."

"Wait. You can't leave." Michael pushed around her brother. "Dinner is ready."

"Maybe he feels uncomfortable with the fact that you brought my ex-partner to dinner," Flex barked. "Have you ever thought of that?"

Lincoln latched on to the excuse. "Yeah. I think, uh, I need to go for a drive to, uh, clear my head. This is just too much for me right now."

"There you go," Flex said.

"Please, Trey, don't go." Michael rushed over to him and tried to take him by the hand.

He stepped back and looked to Flex. "I expect for you to handle this before I return." His eyes narrowed to make his meaning clear.

"I didn't think what this would do to you. We just thought—"

"That's the problem," Flex hissed. "You're always going behind people's backs and trying to fix things."

Michael looked frantic. "Okay, I was wrong, but don't leave. I can fix this, I swear."

"Didn't you hear a word I just said?" Flex pulled her around and signaled for Lincoln to make his get-away. "I don't want you fixing things!"

Lincoln slipped quickly out the door. He signed the papers from the stunned delivery driver and hurried off with the keys.

"No one is ever going to believe this," Lincoln said, sliding behind the wheel. He started the car the same time he saw the house door open. "Get out of here. Get out of here," he chanted, and threw the car in reverse just as Sheldon's bulging belly came into view.

He laughed to himself. "This is crazy. Crazy." The ride to Peyton's house took all of one minute, but he was pleased to see he'd made it there before Peyton returned. Now he just hoped one of those crazy sisters didn't hop into a car and try to follow him— though, at this point, he wouldn't be too surprised if they did.

Lincoln exhaled a long breath and laid his head back against the headrest. The day's events replayed in his mind, and then suddenly he was laughing. "Me, Flex's boyfriend. Give me a break."

The sound of an approaching car ended his laugh-fest, and for a brief moment he feared it would be the meddling triplets, coming to hog-tie and drag him back to dinner.

Instead, he recognized the figure behind a black Mercedes and his heart leaped with excitement.

When she shut off her engine, they both climbed out of their cars.

"I can't believe it," Peyton said, rushing around her car. "You're finally here." She jumped into his arms.

Lincoln caught her and twirled her around in his arms. "Ah, you're a sight for sore eyes." He slid her down the length of his body and then accepted her soft lips in a tantalizing kiss.

Peyton moaned and wrapped her arms around his neck.

Once the kiss ended, her eyes twinkled as she whispered against his lips, "I hope you've packed a lot of energy bars, big boy. You're going to need them tonight."

He laughed. "You do a lot of trash talking for a little girl." He swatted her on the butt and she quickly popped him in the stomach.

"Watch who you're calling a girl." She pulled out of his arms and winked. "You better believe that I'm all woman."

"Thank God for that," he said, following her toward the house. At least the night held more promise.

"Welcome to my hacienda," Peyton announced, as she led the way across the threshold.

Lincoln glanced around and was impressed by the immaculate home. They passed the small foyer and stepped into the living room. Everywhere he looked were beautiful paintings or intriguing sculptures. The whole setting gave him a better insight to this magnificent woman.

"You have a lovely home," he said. "It's also very clean. Sort of tells me not to invite you to my place until I hire a cleaning woman."

"Not very domesticated?" she asked, moving to stand next to him.

"I can work a vacuum, if that's what you're asking." His gaze fell to her lips again and then to her curvy body. "I have a feeling that by the time morning comes, I'm going to need either an ambulance or a priest."

She smiled. "I have a first-aid kit and a Bible. You're going to have to make do." Peyton pulled him down by his shirt and stole a quick kiss. "But before we jump to dessert, I have some bad news," she said.

"Oh?" His hands caressed her hips.

"I didn't cook," she admitted. "So I'm going to run up to my father's and sneak some lasagna from them."

"No!'

Peyton blinked at his sudden outburst. "Is there a problem?"

"I, uh, I'm not too crazy about lasagna," he said, and took some comfort in the fact that it wasn't a lie.

"Oh?" She frowned. "I didn't know that. Then I guess we have a bigger problem than I thought."

"How about we order a pizza?" he suggested.

"A pizza? It's not exactly a romantic dinner."

"Says who? Pizza is perfect for any occasion."

"That is such a 'man' thing to say," she said with a sly smile.

"If it looks like a man, walks like a man, and talks like a man—then chances are you got yourself a man." He smiled and pulled her pliant body against him. "Besides, I'm hungry for something other than food."

"Hmm. Is that right? You go for three months without laying a finger on me and now—"

"The time is right," he finished for her.

"I tell you what. I'll order the pizza and you can grab your luggage." She turned away from him.

He blinked. "Luggage?"

She laughed and glanced over her shoulder. "Yeah,

you know those things you pack before going on a trip?"

"I, uh, the, uh, airlines lost my bags." Now he was lying.

"You poor thing. You really have had a bad day."

Lincoln laughed. "You just have no idea."

Chapter 23

Peyton was surprised by how nervous she was about this evening. After all the erotic dreams, teasing, and trash talk, it all boiled down to tonight. While she called her favorite pizzeria, Lincoln took a shower.

"Nothing is going to ruin this night," she affirmed, hanging up. Giddy with excitement, she sprinted throughout the house and lit every candle she could find. Once that task was completed, she rushed out to her car and grabbed a bag of rose petals she'd purchased from her local florist.

She sprinkled the petals throughout the house, but dumped most of them around and on the bed. At the sound of the shower shutting off, she made one last dash to the kitchen to deliberate over which wine would work best with their dinner.

"It's a perfect fit," Lincoln announced, joining her in the kitchen in an imperial kimono robe. "Where did you get this?"

"Kanji, an artist I represent, had a show out in Tokyo a few months ago and brought back all kinds

of things. I thought this would be perfect for you."
She grabbed a merlot. "Do you like it?"

He eased up behind her and whispered against
her ear, "I'll love anything you give me."

"Ooh?" She grinned as his hands slid around her
waist.

Simultaneously, the phone and the doorbell rang.

Lincoln kissed the back of her head. "I'll get the
door."

"And I'll get the phone."

"Make sure you unplug it when you're through,"
he said, as he hurried out of the kitchen.

"You got it." Her grin remained wide as she
reached for the phone. "Hello."

Michael's low voice hissed over the line. "P.J., it's a
disaster!"

Peyton instantly knew what her sister was referring
to. "I take it that dinner isn't going too well?" she
asked cheerfully.

"Don't gloat. Help us figure out a way to fix this.
When Morgan showed up, Trey stormed out, and
Flex isn't talking to us."

"I told you something like this would happen.
When are you going to learn your lesson?" Peyton
looked to see Lincoln racing through the house.

"I need to get my wallet," he informed her as he
breezed past the breakfast bar.

"Who's that?" Michael asked.

"Don't worry about who it is. You have enough
problems right now. Where did Trey go?"

Lincoln passed again, holding up his wallet.

"How in the hell should I know? I think he and
Flex were already having problems before they got
here. He snapped at Flex once at the airport, and
then when we first arrived at the house they were up
in the guest room for a long time talking pretty loud.

I couldn't hear what they were saying because Dad wouldn't let us go up and listen against the door."

Peyton slumped her head into her hand. "Just great, Mike. Where is Flex now?"

Michael's voice dropped even lower. "At the dinner table. It took forever to get him there, and now no one is talking. Morgan looks put out—"

"Of course he's put out," Peyton snapped. "I'm sure he's been able to figure out that he's been set up by the idiot sisters."

Lincoln approached the breakfast bar with their box dinner. He winked at her and signaled for her to hurry off the phone.

Peyton nodded. "Look, Mike. Why don't you just put everyone out of their misery and ask Morgan to leave?" She noticed Lincoln's frown and placed her hand over the receiver to whisper, "I'll be just a moment."

He flashed a quick smile and then eased onto a stool.

"Look, this is your mess. I don't want my name brought up. Hell, I wouldn't be surprised if Flex and Trey skip out on the wedding and head back to Georgia."

Michael's voiced filled with shock. "So you're turning your back on us?"

"Look, you, Sheldon, and Frankie are like the *Titanic*. I'm not climbing on board. Apologize to everyone, ask Morgan to leave, and pray you haven't ruined Flex's and Trey's relationship. Now I have to go."

"I just remembered," Michael said. "Aren't you supposed to still be waiting for Lincoln in San Francisco?"

"Good-bye, Mike." She hung up and rolled her eyes. "Let me warn you now: my sisters are crazy."

"You don't say?" His smile wobbled. "But let's not let them ruin our night." He popped open the pizza box and inhaled. "Citarella has nothing on this."

Peyton smiled. "And to jazz it up, we're having wine." She held up the bottle and then grabbed two glasses from the freezer.

He winked. "Where should we go?"

"Let's start in the living room and hopefully work our way back." When she bounded out of the kitchen, he followed close on her heels.

Minutes later, they made themselves comfortable on a small pallet among a circle of rose petals on the floor.

"Let me ask you a question," Lincoln said, as he wolfed down his first slice of pizza. "Do you think we're ready for tonight?"

The question surprised her. "What do you mean?"

"I mean us. How do you feel about us?"

She smiled through the tightening of her heart muscles. "I have to admit I never thought I'd see the day when I would find someone like you.

"The last few days, I've done little else but analyze everything we've done, everything we've said in the last three months. Trust me, I've tried to find something wrong with what we have going. I know that sounds weird, but that's pretty much how I've operated until now."

"So what are my test results?" he asked softly.

She hesitated before she admitted, "So far so good."

"I'll accept that," Lincoln said, and then glanced around. "If I didn't know any better, I'd say that you were trying to seduce me," he added as he played with the rose petals.

"Is it working?"

"Maybe." He gave her a light shrug. "You know I do have to warn you: I'm not exactly easy."

Her brows twitched upward. "Oh? You mean to tell me after the flowers and wine you're not going to give it up?"

He grinned and took a sip of his wine. "What if you don't respect me in the morning?"

"Oh, baby." Her gaze absorbed his. "You don't ever have to worry about that."

"Really?" He lowered his second slice of pizza and leaned forward.

With her head already light from the alcohol, the potency of his kiss caused her to drift blissfully among the clouds in her mind. She heard the pizza box being pushed aside as he crawled above her and she lowered herself onto her back.

This is it. She mentally prepared herself.

The feathery touch of his hand drifted up the center of her chest and her entire body quivered. The kiss consumed her, but she gave back as fiercely as she received.

She had no memory of her clothes being removed, and as far as she was concerned they'd melted off. When his hot mouth left her body, he scorched a trail of tiny, biting kisses down the length of her neck and along the curvy plane of her shoulders.

With a husky sigh, Peyton closed her eyes, caught in the sensuality that radiated from Lincoln. And then just as quickly, he took her mouth again in another sweet, intoxicating kiss.

However, not to miss out on a chance to do her own exploring, she roamed her hands along his rock-hard chest, and then dipped them inside his silk kimono. Vast mounds of creamy flesh and rippling muscles greeted her fingertips. A surge of power emboldened her moves and her hand drifted downward.

Lincoln was a large man.

The moment she glided her hands along his shaft, there was a slight change in his breathing. She stroked him again, reveling in the soft groan that fell from his lips. Tightening her hand around him, she picked up the tempo.

His lips parted as Lincoln buried his head against the crook of her neck. "Jesus," he whispered.

Still heady with power, Peyton gently eased him over onto his side, and then farther onto his back. She made quick work of pushing everything out of the way, before she took great pleasure in climbing this Mt. Everest of a man.

"Be gentle," he joked.

"Don't tell me that you're already begging for mercy." With one tug, his robe belt came undone and every inch of his body was exposed. "Impressive."

"Beautiful," he whispered as his gaze roamed over her. With dreamlike slowness, his hand curved around one of her firm breasts and then gave the erect nipple a slight pinch.

Peyton drew a sharp breath and arched against his hand. He repeated the performance on her other breast until she filled her lungs to their full capacity and began to tremble.

Lincoln leaned her forward and then took a nipple gently between his teeth. Her nipples hardened even more as his tongue and lips tugged at her in a loving caress that made her moan. She had no choice but to succumb to the heat that twisted and melted through her.

She felt as if she were on fire when his teeth closed around her again. It was harder this time, and forced an intense sound of pleasure from parts of her she'd long forgotten. Belatedly, she felt his hand snake in between her legs, and before she could prepare herself, two long fingers dipped inside her silky walls.

Her warmth was an incredible turn-on. It took everything Lincoln had not to just toss her beneath him and have his way with her. Above everything, he wanted to take his time with her.

Slowly, gently, he stroked the walls of her moist cave while he worshiped her magnificent breasts. He listened to her labored breathing as she rocked her hips against his hand. It was like heaven, feeling the way she quaked in his arms, and as a bonus he caressed her feminine bud with the pad of his thumb.

Peyton's slight rocking transformed into a hard pound. Lincoln's excitement grew at the feel of her muscles tightening and loosening like an accelerated heartbeat.

Air rushed from Peyton's body as an orgasmic cry tore itself from her body and she shuddered convulsively. She fell against him and tried to gain control of her breathing.

Lincoln smiled and kissed the two mounds pressed against his face. "That was a nice warm-up," he said.

"I'd say." She laughed and then rolled off of him.

"Where are you going?" He curled onto his side. "I thought we agreed that there would be no breaks."

Peyton sat up and reached for her glass from off the coffee table. "I just wanted a sip of wine, that's all."

"Uh-huh." Lincoln climbed up from off the floor and stood above her. "Maybe it's time we take this to the bedroom."

"Or—" She twinkled a smile up at him and shifted onto her knees. "We can try something else."

Before her meaning sank in, he watched as she took his erect shaft into her hands and glided it into her hot mouth. Instant, intense pleasure assaulted Lincoln. Despite his desire to roll his eyes to the back of his head, he also wanted to watch how her mouth slid lovingly over his throbbing arousal. There was nothing more exquisite than this: her tongue, the walls of her mouth, and her exceptional ability to take him in so deep that made her an exceptional woman.

With his eyes still glued on her performance, Lincoln

slid his fingers through her hair, but was careful not to guide her head. Then he made a sound deep in his throat.

In response of him possibly losing control, Peyton upped the ante by quickening her strokes. His hips matched her pace and soon his moans became groans and even a few curses.

At last, he backed away and smiled down at her. "You're trying to kill me."

"Not quite." She stood up and approached him. "But I have the skills to back up everything I told you."

"Then it's off to the bedroom." Lincoln swept her up into his arms and grabbed his wallet from the coffee table.

Peyton giggled. "What about your ankle?"

"There's no disabled list in this game, remember?"

She slipped her arms around his neck. "In that case, batter up."

The phone rang.

Lincoln stopped. "I thought you turned it off."

"Ignore it. Trust me, it's just Larry, Curly, or Moe," she joked.

"Are you sure?"

She kissed him, and then challenged, "Is this your way of trying to get a break?"

"It's time I shut you up." He winked and carried her off toward the bedroom.

The eager new lovers came together with an overwhelming desire and a ravishing hunger. For Peyton, she couldn't touch enough or kiss enough to sate this need for him. And the things he could do with his mouth were definitely a sin.

Limp from her second orgasm, it took everything Peyton had not to beg for a moment to catch her breath. If she did, he would have undoubtedly held it over her head for eternity.

"I can't wait any longer," Lincoln panted as he staked the dominant position. "I need to be inside you."

In that moment, her energy restored itself and her desire increased tenfold.

From above her head, Lincoln reached for his wallet and withdrew a condom. Out of the corner of her eye, she noted the magnum wrapper and smiled. She took pleasure in assisting him, but as he eased inside her, everything changed.

At the feel of Peyton's tight muscles trying to adjust to his size, Lincoln was certain that he was about to come unglued. He ground his teeth as her heat pulsed around him and he still refused to give up control.

To his surprise, she didn't protest or ask for mercy. She simply tightened her legs around his hips and enabled him to sink deeper. When she finally took all of him and he'd allowed sufficient time for her body to adjust, she surprised him by raining light kisses down his face.

"I'm ready," she whispered.

Lincoln swore that there were no sweeter words in the dictionary as he began to move. "Please let me know if I'm hurting you."

In answer, Peyton's hips matched his rhythm. He took his time, wanting this moment to last. But after long minutes of slow, measured strokes, it grew harder to resist his building orgasm.

Peyton thrashed madly beneath him, oblivious to all space and time. She was slave to the wild sensations coursing through her. She wanted it to go on forever, but something sparked within her and thrust her toward an earth-shattering climax.

Stroke by stroke, control ebbed from Lincoln. With each silky contraction of her body, he moaned her name and confessed his love until at long last his throttled howl merged with her cries of ecstasy. Together they drowned in the sweet rain of their release.

Every tender emotion Peyton had ever experienced swirled inside her. She wiped at her eyes, not remembering when tears had slid from them. It had been more than worth the small wait for this night, and Lincoln had been worth all the frogs she'd ever kissed.

He was perfect for her. She had said that many times in the last ninety days, and tonight he proved it to her once again. More than anything she wanted this man permanently in her life, but she was too afraid to hope for that.

He rolled over onto his side and pulled her close. "Would you think any less of me if—"

"We took a break?" she suggested.

"Well, I'm not saying that I need one or anything."

"No, no," she said. "Of course not. I mean, I was just thinking—"

"That you wanted one, too?"

"Me? No, you look as though you might need one," she said.

He propped himself up on his elbows. "Who, me? I can go another round right now. Come here."

Peyton held up her hands. "Mercy, mercy. Dear God, mercy. I need a minute," she confessed.

Lincoln plopped down on the pillow. "Oh, thank God."

Chapter 24

Lincoln and Peyton woke to the sound of a ringing phone. Neither of them wanted to pry their limbs from the warm cocoon they'd created after their last round of lovemaking. However, the ringing persisted.

"I don't believe this," Peyton moaned, and rolled out of Lincoln's embrace.

"What time is it?" Lincoln glanced around.

"It's kill my sisters time," she grumbled, snatching the phone. "This better be good," she warned the caller.

Michael's voice trembled over the line. "He hasn't come back. It's nearly midnight and Trey hasn't returned."

Peyton sat up. "What?"

"I don't know what to do. Flex is in his room and refuses to come out."

Peyton was beginning to feel the steady pounding of a migraine. "Did you at least get rid of Morgan?"

Lincoln moved next to her and began caressing one of her breasts with light gentle strokes.

"Morgan left hours ago," Michael said in a quivering voice. "Peyton, you have to come and help us talk to Flex. He may never forgive us for this. What if something's happened to Trey?"

Lincoln snuggled closer and drew a taut nipple into his mouth.

Peyton smiled as her eyes drifted closed. Her body was tingling again. She lost herself for a moment and moaned into the phone.

"Are you listening to me, P.J.? What are you doing?"

"Mike, this really isn't a good time." She curled toward Lincoln and slid her hands through his short hair.

"C'mon, Peyton. You and Flex are close. He'll talk to you."

Lincoln slid a hand beneath the sheet and nudged her legs open.

"Sheldon thinks we should call the police."

Peyton was jolted out of the mood and closed her legs. "The police?"

Lincoln also sat up, just as another shrilling filled the room. He glanced around.

Peyton placed a hand over the receiver to whisper, "What is that?"

Huffing, Lincoln pulled back the covers to climb out of bed. "I think it's my cell phone."

"Is that your little friend?" Michael asked. "Tell him I said hi."

"Are you for real?" Peyton shoved the rest of the sheets from off her body and also stood from the bed.

Lincoln finally reached his folded pants and dug out his cell phone. "Hello."

"Psst," Peyton hissed. "I'm going to take this call up front. "I'll keep it short." She slipped into a robe and rushed out of the room.

"Linc, Linc. Are you there?"

"Yeah, I'm here. Who's this?" He sat in some kind of lounge chair.

"It's Flex. Look, I need you to get back over here. My sisters are going crazy. They think something has happened to you. They're not leaving here until you come back."

"What? You're supposed to be telling them the truth." Lincoln glanced up to make sure that Peyton hadn't come back into the room.

"I swear, I was going to, but things just kept escalating. Morgan stayed through dinner and I couldn't tell them the truth when he was here. It would have looked like I brought you here to make him jealous or something."

Lincoln's mouth fell open. "I can't believe I'm having this conversation."

"I'll tell them, but not now. Mike has worked herself up into a frenzy because you're gone. Sheldon went home mainly because she's supposed to be on bed rest."

"Then tell them I'm at Peyton's house. You know her—she's my *girlfriend*."

"If I go downstairs now and tell them that I haven't been upset the whole night about your leaving and that I've gotten them all worked up over nothing, I'll have a mob on my hands."

Lincoln stood and crept to the bathroom for more privacy. Once he closed the door, he hissed into the phone, "And what do you think will happen tomorrow when I'm introduced as Peyton's boyfriend? Either way, you're between a rock and a hard place."

"Don't make me beg. I need you here," Flex panted. "To make matters worse, apparently Michael also sent Morgan an invitation to the wedding. I can't go to the wedding without a date now. First of all, he'll think you've dumped me and I'll look even more pathetic in his eyes. Who wants to be a two-time loser?"

Lincoln pulled the phone away and stared at it for a moment before he brought it back against his ear. "Are you even listening to yourself? I'm not about to be Peyton *and* your date. In fact, when I hang up I'm going to forget that we ever had this conversation."

"Linc, don't hang up."

"Tell them the truth."

"I need more time. Please, they're talking about calling the police and filing a missing person report."

"Flex—"

"Twenty minutes. Just show up, let them know that you're okay, and once they go home you can slip back over to Peyton's."

"Flex—"

"Just this one favor and I swear I'll leave you alone."

Lincoln released a frustrated sigh. "I must be out of my mind."

"After this, Linc, we're square."

Over the years, Lincoln had prided himself on being a good friend to people. There was nothing like being there for friends who needed a shoulder to cry on, a sofa to crash on, and even a loan of some gas money until next payday; but this was above the call of duty—by anyone's standards.

"Linc?"

"Twenty minutes," he said, and then squeezed his eyes shut. He couldn't believe he was about to do this.

Flex exhaled. "Thank you, Linc. You're a good friend."

"Gee, thanks."

* * *

Peyton sat on the sofa with her legs tucked beneath her and the cordless phone cradled between her shoulder and chin. On a night that was filled with such incredible highs, the last thing she wanted to do was try to counsel her loony sisters about respecting other people's boundaries.

She believed that Frankie and Michael were simply trying to help, but they had a habit of going about things the wrong way. "Where is Flex now?"

"Upstairs in his room," Michael said. "He won't talk to us."

"Imagine that."

"This isn't funny, P.J. Can't you just come over for a few minutes and see if you can talk to him? You two have always been close."

"Primarily because I know how to keep my nose out of his business. Just let him sleep on this. You'll see. He'll be a lot better in the morning."

"No. We're not leaving here until Trey comes back," Michael insisted. "How can we? We're responsible for him running out of here like that."

"Since it's so late, maybe he's checked into some hotel somewhere. You're staying there isn't helping anything."

"He hasn't checked into a hotel. His luggage is still here in the foyer. Please, P.J., come over for a few minutes."

"Absolutely not. I have company and—" she stopped and looked up as Lincoln suddenly appeared fully dressed. She placed her hand over the receiver. "Where are you going?"

Lincoln drew a breath and appeared either nervous or uncomfortable. "I'm just going to run out for a few minutes."

"Why?" She unfolded her legs.

"No. Don't get up. I'm just going to run to a convenience store for, uh, something for a headache."

"I'm not wearing you out, am I?" She winked and then watched as his adorable dimples made an appearance.

"Don't brag. I'll be right back."

"Wait. I have plenty of Ibuprofen and Tylenol."

His smile disappeared as quickly as it came. "Uh, I also need to pick up some, uh . . ."

Peyton frowned.

"Condoms!" He brightened suddenly. "Yeah, some more condoms. I'm all out."

Peyton pressed her hand tighter against the receiver as her face warmed from embarrassment. The last thing she wanted her sisters to overhear was about their condom deficit.

"Oh, okay." She smiled. "Do you want me to come with you?"

Lincoln walked over to her and then leaned down to brush a kiss against her lips. "No, that's not necessary. You finish talking to your sister. I'll be right back."

"But do you know where—"

"I'll find it." He turned away, but stopped before he left the living room. "You just make sure you stay right here. I want you to be ready when I get back."

"You got it," she whispered and placed the phone back against her ear.

"Peyton, are you still there?" Michael asked.

"Yeah, I'm back." She sighed and daydreamed about the man who had just left. Her mind was consumed with Lincoln's broad muscles, excessively wicked tongue, and impressive . . . anatomy.

"Mike, can I ask you a question?" she asked, cutting her sister off in midsentence. "When did you know that Phil was the one for you?"

Michael's sputtering made it clear that the question caught her off guard. "The one?"

She started to elaborate when common sense

kicked in and reminded her whom she was talking to. "Nothing. Just forget it."

Of course, she wasn't able to get off that easy. "Oh my God, Frankie," Michael yelled. "Pick up the other phone. P.J. is in love."

Faster than a speeding bullet, there was a click and Frankie's excited voice filled the line. "You've got to be kidding. Is it this Lincoln guy?"

She should deny it, Peyton realized, but she couldn't. Instead, she made a confession. "Girls, I really think I've finally found my Price Charming."

Chapter 25

Joey removed her jacket as she entered her father's home and then greeted Frankie with a tentative hug. "Where is he?"

"In his old bedroom," Frankie said shakily. "Oh, Joe. We really screwed things up. We only wanted to make Morgan jealous and show how Flex has moved on. We thought he'd love it."

Joey shook her head. "When are you girls going to learn? We don't want you guys constantly trying to fix everyone's lives." She headed for the staircase.

"*We?* You've been known to poke your nose in where it doesn't belong a few times, yourself." Frankie followed her. "We were just trying to help. If Flex put Morgan in his place, then maybe he wouldn't feel like he needed to be so far from home."

"No one is saying that you don't have good intentions. You just need to learn when to draw the line. Where is Michael?"

"Michael is on the phone with Peyton in the living room and Dad is around here somewhere."

Joey shook her head and drew a deep breath when

she reached Flex's bedroom door. "Give me a few minutes alone with him."

"Maybe I should stay for support?"

Joey stared at her.

"Or I could just join Michael downstairs." Frankie backed up. "Just call me if you need any help."

Joey rolled her eyes and knocked softly on her brother's door. "Flex, are you in there?"

"Will you girls just let it go?" Frustration saturated his voice.

"Flex, it's me, Joey."

He didn't respond.

"Look, I'm on your side. I just want to talk to you for a few minutes." When he didn't respond, she added, "I'm alone."

The door clicked and then slowly opened. At her first glance at her brother, the deep-grooved lines in his face bothered her. It made him look older— tired.

"C'mon in."

She stared at him for a second, and then entered the room. "How are you holding up?"

"Are you kidding? I feel like a prisoner or, at the very least, a grounded teenager." He closed the door and started pacing like a caged animal.

Joey sat down on the edge of the bed. "I guess you're pretty upset about Trey leaving?"

"Hardly."

"You know Frankie and Michael didn't mean—" She stopped when she finally caught what he'd said. "Excuse me?"

"Everyone is making a mountain out of a mole hill."

"So . . . you're not upset?" She struggled to understand. "Were you and Trey having some kind of trouble before you arrived?"

"No. We were actually getting along fine before today, thank you." His pacing increased.

"I don't understand." Joey stood up. "Are you or aren't you mad your boyfriend stormed out of here after Frankie and Michael ambushed you?"

"I'm mad about the ambush," he affirmed, while the muscles along his jaw twitched. "I felt like an idiot in front of Morgan. On top of that, I froze when I saw him—and in front of my family. It was humiliating."

As a firefighter and as a man, Joey had deduced a long time ago that showing weakness or vulnerability was some kind of cardinal sin. After Morgan had walked out of their ten-year relationship, Flex did all he could to camouflage his emotions. Even now, she sensed the war within him raging on.

"And what about Trey?" she asked. "Why aren't you concerned about him? He was ambushed, too, and he has been gone for hours. Does he even know anyone else here in town?"

"Trust me. He's not lacking for company at the moment." Flex looked at her again and his demeanor changed. "You know, you should go now. I'm fine. This whole thing will blow over."

She shrugged. "It's okay. I'll probably just hang out with Frankie and Michael until Trey comes back. They really do want to apologize to him."

Their conversation was interrupted at the sudden knock at the door.

"Go away," Flex barked. "Uh, Joey, about your staying—"

"Joey, come get on the phone," Frankie's excited voice boomed through the door. "It's about P.J."

Joey turned to her brother. "It sounds like they've already found a new victim."

Flex visibly relaxed. "Thank God."

* * *

"What in the hell am I doing?" Lincoln asked as he started the car. He ignored the fact his stomach had twisted into a large knot, but it was harder to ease his conscience about deceiving Peyton's family.

The whole ride back to the Adams home, Lincoln convinced himself that silence was golden. The way he was beginning to see it, as long as no one asked him about his relationship with Flex, then *technically* he wasn't lying.

His mood brightened.

This was Flex's mess. Up until a few hours ago, he had no idea of the deception that was in play. So there was still a way for him to walk away clean.

Lincoln parked and climbed out of the car. *Whatever you do, don't lie,* he coached himself; but despite the small pep talk, the knot tightened in his gut.

Taking a deep breath, he started up the walkway.

"Glad to see the girls haven't chased you off for good."

Lincoln stopped and turned toward the voice. "Mr. Adams?" Lincoln swallowed when he made out the man's silhouette from off the porch deck. "What are you doing out here?"

Marlin stepped from out of the shadows and into the porch's pool of light. "The problem with having so many daughters is that they have a tendency to take over the household from time to time." He shrugged, with a wide smile. "Most times, I don't mind."

Lincoln smiled. "You have wonderful daughters."

"And a pretty terrific son."

After a slight pause, Lincoln found his voice again. "He's certainly a good guy. Saved my neck."

Marlin nodded. "Would you like to have a seat out here with me for a little chat? Once you go inside, I'm afraid I won't be able to get a word in edgewise."

Lincoln didn't like that idea. "Actually, I think I—"

"Oh, c'mon." Marlin approached and slapped a hand against Lincoln's back. "I'm not going to bite you."

Horror-stricken, Lincoln wondered if the man would become alarmed if he started hollering for help. "Sure. I'd be glad talk to you for a few minutes," he said instead.

"Good, good."

A few seconds later, Lincoln found himself sitting on a porch swing, and avoiding meeting Mr. Adams's gaze.

"I hope you forgive me," Marlin said, hesitantly. "I'm not used to doing this sort of thing, but, uh, I guess I should start off by saying that I'm glad you and Francis came for the wedding."

Someone just shoot me and put me out of my misery.
"I'm happy I could come."

Marlin cleared his throat. "Well, I don't know how much Francis has told you about our relationship, but it's a bit strained at the moment."

"Actually, sir, he hasn't talked to me in any real detail about your relationship. That sort of thing isn't really any of my business." The silence that followed forced Lincoln to glance over at the older man. Was he crying? "Mr. Adams?"

Marlin shook his head. "He's probably still hurt about the ugly things I said to him when I'd found out the truth behind him and Morgan being more than just *roommates*."

Lincoln bolted to his feet. "Mr. Adams, I think you need to have this conversation with Francis—I mean, Flex."

Marlin stood up as well. "Please call me Marlin. Heck, you're dating one of my kids, right?"

Lincoln swallowed. "Right."

"C'mon, sit back down." Marlin reclaimed his seat

and patted a spot beside him. "It's time I get a lot of this off my chest."

"Then let me go in and get Flex. He's the one you need to be talking to."

"But what if he doesn't listen?" Marlin's shoulders slumped. "You saw how he was in the car. He won't give me the chance to prove that I've changed. I've been reading up on all of this gay stuff. Heck, I even watch that *Will and Grace* show. It's pretty funny," he said, chuckling.

It was impossible for Lincoln to ignore the fact that the man was trying hard to understand something he quite simply didn't get. "Mr. Adams— Marlin. From my own experience, one of the hardest things for me to do is to talk to my father. He's a good man, much like you; but when it comes to communicating, neither of us is very good at it. Whenever I talk, he's hearing something else and vice versa. But maybe the problem we *all* have is that we're trying to talk at the same time. No one's listening. Maybe all Flex wants is for you to listen."

Marlin lowered his head to stare at his braided fingers. "I think you might have something there."

Lincoln exhaled, feeling the revelation of his own words and vowing to spend more time with his own father. "I'll go inside and get your son for you."

"Thanks, Trey." Marlin stood once again. "You know, you're all right. I like you."

"I hope you remember that tomorrow." Lincoln returned to the front door and entered the house.

"Maybe I'm just reading way too much into this," Peyton said. "Everyone knows that long-distance relationships don't work. And it's not like he's even suggested that we—" She stopped. "I'm going around in circles, aren't I?"

Frankie sighed. "He really has gotten to you, hasn't he?"

"We definitely have to meet this one," Michael added.

"Only if you guys promise to be on your best behavior," Peyton said, laughing. "None of this showing up to dinner with Ricky or something."

"Low blow," Michael said.

Joey giggled. "Well, I've met Lincoln and I'm not surprised by this. Just make sure you continue to play it cool. Remember your rule about never showing a guy your complete hand."

Peyton smiled and drew a breath. "You know, the thing about Lincoln and me is that neither of us is into head games. We say what we mean and mean what we say. It's refreshing."

"He's also a challenge," Joey added.

"There's that, too." Peyton nodded. Still nestled on the sofa, she'd refilled her wineglass and she enjoyed the wine's light, smooth taste while her mind danced with thoughts of Lincoln.

"Do you think it's too forward to ask him where we are in the relationship? You know to, sort of, check and see if we're on the same page? After all, it's only been a few months."

"Sure. There are plenty of couples who have gotten hitched in less time than that," Frankie said.

"And some of us take a little longer," Michael amended.

"Oh, I'm not saying I'm ready to get married again," Peyton protested.

"But you've thought about it," Joey said softly. "Admit it."

Peyton didn't trust herself to speak. At this moment, she was operating completely on emotion, which was always a dangerous thing to do. "I'm all out of wisecracks," she admitted. "I don't have a list of things I can't stand or even one of things I'd like to change. Is this what it's like to be sprung?"

Michael laughed. "Damn. Exactly what did he do to you over there?"

Peyton laughed. "I'll never tell."

The good news was that Frankie and Michael didn't ambush Lincoln when he walked in through the door. He did, however, hear their excited voices somewhere toward the living room area while he snuck up the stairs.

Once he reached the second level, he crept down to the guest room and knocked.

"What is it now?" Flex called out.

"It's me," Lincoln hissed back. "Open the door." Immediately, it was jerked open.

"It's about time you got back here," Flex said with a measure of relief. "What are you trying to do, give me a heart attack?"

"Me?" Lincoln stepped into the room. "In case I haven't made this clear, I really resent this whole situation. And furthermore, I can't believe you—my relationship guru—won't step up to the plate and just clear all this mess up."

"I was going to . . . until Morgan showed up."

"Yeah, I remember—I was there." He crossed his arms. "You froze. What was that all about?"

Flex's shoulders slumped as he exhaled. "I don't know."

Lincoln watched the transformation of his friend, fully aware that this was a side of Flex he'd never witnessed before. This giant of a man so clearly had a softer and deeper side to him.

"Look," Lincoln began again. "I think I understand why you didn't want to say anything in front of your ex. Clearly, there's still a lot of hurt between you two. And let's face it, I look good on anybody's arm," he joked to lighten the mood.

Flex laughed.

"But," Lincoln continued, "you should at least tell your family the truth. I was just seconds away from the 'why do you want my son's hand?' speech from your dad."

Flex sat on the bed. "The mere fact that I lied about being in a relationship will only come off as a cry for help to my sisters. And I just don't know if I can handle them trying to *fix* me right now."

"They just love you . . ." Lincoln hesitated. "And so does your dad. You should go talk to him."

The tension immediately returned to Flex's features. "We're not going there. I only came for the wedding. I said all I had to say to him before I moved to Atlanta."

Lincoln nodded and began to feel he'd done all he could here. "Okay, so it's none of my business, but I think you're making a mistake. I was just talking to your dad outside and, yes, he may be struggling with certain things, but he's trying—and he's your dad."

"Linc, you don't know anything about this."

"Maybe not, but forgive me for saying this, but it seems to me that you have to shoulder a lot of the blame on this."

"Me?"

"You weren't entirely truthful with your dad about your relationship with Morgan, were you? It's kind of like how you're not being honest now. You lied . . . for ten years. Of course, he blew up. I don't know what was said and I don't want to know. However, the man I just finished talking to may have a lot of regrets, but he loves you. Go talk to him."

"I can't." Flex sat on the edge of the bed.

"A man who runs into burning buildings for a living can do anything. I know." Lincoln turned toward the door.

"Wait."

Lincoln drew a deep breath and slowly exhaled. "Look, I sympathize with you. I wish I could help you, but I can't." He turned for the door.

"Where are you going?"

"Back to Peyton's—where I belong." Lincoln's shoulders slumped. "I'm falling in love with a woman I haven't been completely honest with either. I waited for this trip to tell her that I know you. I didn't tell her, because she'd vowed never to date a friend of yours again. I didn't tell you for the same reason."

Flex exhaled. "I guess I gave you some pretty lousy advice."

"It wasn't so bad. I'm pretty sure she'll understand—just like your family will understand."

Flex nodded and then slowly lifted his gaze. "Falling in love?"

Lincoln's face exploded into a smile. "I'm crazy about her. I have been since the moment I laid eyes on her. We just fit—intellectually, spiritually, and physically."

"Hey, hey." Flex held up his hands. "Too much information."

"It's true," Lincoln continued. "I'm in love with your sister, which is the main reason why I have to break up with you by tomorrow. Peyton is bringing me over for lunch. Either you tell everyone the truth or I will."

"Wait!" Flex stopped him. "You better go out the window. Joey's out there."

Lincoln rolled his eyes. Could it get any worse?

Chapter 26

"Where have you been?" Peyton asked the moment Lincoln walked through the door. She ran a hand through her fly away hair and then tossed her keys on a table by the front door. "I was just about to go out and look for you."

Lincoln hesitated with the truth. "I had to help out a friend. Sorry. I thought you were probably still on the phone with your sisters."

She blinked. "A friend? You know someone out here?"

"It's true what they say—it's a small world." Turning on his best puppy-dog expression, he closed the distance between them. "Sorry, I worried you." He pulled her into his arms.

Peyton drew a breath and relaxed. "I was having crazy thoughts of you being a carjacking victim."

He chuckled. "You're not going to get rid of me that easily. Besides"—he reached inside his jacket—"I brought reinforcements." He held up a pack of condoms.

She chuckled. "Is that your way of getting out of trouble?"

"Depends."

"On what?"

"On whether it's working." He grinned and then leaned down to steal a kiss. He could tell all was forgotten by the way she leaned into him and draped her arms around his neck.

Feeling every bit the gallant hero, Lincoln swept her up into his arms and proceeded to carry her back to the bedroom. In bed, their clothes were removed in a wild flurry of movements and their bodies came together like two perfect pieces in a jigsaw puzzle.

There was something about the sound of her soft whimpers and gentle moans that turned Lincoln into an insatiable animal. He couldn't get enough of how her body molded itself around him or how her lips controlled him.

Beyond certainty, he knew he could never tire of making love to her. This was it, he told himself. This was what he'd been searching for his entire life. Not only was she beautiful, she was intelligent, strong, and devoid of head games.

Lincoln lost himself within her chocolate limbs and her smooth rich taste. Her orgasmic cries heightened in their intensity and her slick walls tightened around him.

An orgasmic cry exploded from her lungs and reverberated off the bedroom walls. Lincoln clutched her close as his body trembled and quaked in the aftermath of his own explosion.

Seconds later, he still held her close while their heavy breathing blended together.

"How do you feel, baby?" he asked.

Peyton moaned. "Please don't tell me that you're ready to go again."

"Tired?" He chuckled.

"You win. You win," she conceded. "I'm a wimp."

"And I'm the what?"

She hesitated.

He cupped his ear and leaned down. "I'm sorry. I didn't hear you."

"Fine." She smacked him playfully in the chest. "You're the king. Are you happy?"

"Extremely." He turned onto his side so he could glance down at her. *What about you?* "How do you feel?"

Her smile softened at the edges. "Honestly?"

He frowned. "Of course."

"Nervous," she said, as if unloading a large burden. "It's been three months and I keep waiting for a ball to drop or for the clock to strike midnight."

Lincoln studied her.

"I know, I know. I'm being silly." She shrugged, but was careful not to meet his gaze. "I'm not being fair to you or to this . . . relationship."

He clutched a hand over his heart. "Oh my God. She finally said it. Quick, someone call the media."

"Very funny." She rolled her eyes. "I just can't believe that things are so good between us."

He studied her again. "Can I ask you a question?"

She drew a nervous breath. "Sure."

"What did this Ricky really do to you?" When she didn't readily respond, he continued. "Dating is difficult. You're not going to get an argument out of me on that. We've shared our horror stories. But . . . you didn't marry just because you thought it was the next step, did you?"

She started to get up, but Lincoln gently held her in place. "Can I tell you what I think?"

Again, she didn't say anything.

"I think you were in love and I think he either pulled a fast one or disappointed you somehow."

After another long pause, she finally spoke. "I should have known better. Lord knows, my family warned me that he was just looking for a free ride. I bought into the whole starving artist spiel. Hell, how could I not? I know plenty of them. The thing is, Ricky never wrote songs, or booked gigs, or tried to get into anyone's studio. Though he did know how to throw a party. Sometimes three or fours times a week.

"So that was our relationship. I worked and he spent all the money. No one wants to admit that they've been made a fool. And it's harder when everyone in the world knows but you. I understand why my brother flew across the country when he and Morgan broke up. Everyone was trying to fix his broken heart . . . as if they could. My three oldest sisters kept setting him up on blind dates."

"What was wrong with that?"

"Nothing, except that they kept forgetting to tell him. Flex kept showing up at restaurants to meet one of us and instead he was met by his date for the evening. He caught on after the second time, then they went to ambushing him."

"Well, I know what that's like."

"What?"

"Oh, nothing." He waved off his comment. "So you and your brother have a lot in common?"

"As far as relationships go, yes. After I filed for divorce, Ricky found himself a richer sugar mama and I was spared paying alimony. Flex wasn't so lucky."

Lincoln frowned. "He had to pay alimony?"

"No. Morgan cleaned out their bank accounts, CDs, and stocks. Flex was devastated."

"Was he?" he asked somberly.

"Yeah. Don't tell my sisters, but I think he made the right choice in leaving. Lord knows I came close to moving to either London or New York myself."

"But that's just running away from the problem. And always expecting men to disappoint you is no way to live. I can't guarantee I'm not going to disappoint you from time to time. You can't guarantee you won't do the same."

She sighed. "I know."

Lincoln directed her chin so that their gazes would meet again. "Do you?"

His intense gaze saw past her facade and peeked into her soul. She didn't mean for the tears to leak from her eyes, and once it happened she suddenly wanted to curl up and hide.

Leaning forward, he kissed the dewy tracks of her tears. "It's okay," he whispered.

And she believed him.

One kiss led to another, while one touch led to another round of lovemaking.

In all honesty, she didn't think she had it in her, but once they got started she begged him not to stop.

Covered in sweat, the lovers had more than their fair share of rose petals sticking to their bodies. However, after adjourning to the bathroom for a hot shower, it wasn't long before Peyton found herself pressed up against the glass orb surrounding the tile.

She didn't have an answer to why she couldn't get enough of him. Maybe it was time to stop asking why or when it was all going to end. Maybe it was time to just enjoy the moment—enjoy everything he made her feel.

She took her time washing him. How could any woman not love the feel of this man's chiseled body for the piece of art that it was? As hard as she tried, it wasn't long before her negative thoughts raced back through her mind.

He would be leaving at the end of the week. Long-distance relationships never worked. And there still has to be something wrong with him.

"What's the matter?" Linc asked, shutting off the shower and reaching for the baby oil.

"Nothing," she lied.

His handsome features twisted into a dubious frown. "It sure looked like more than nothing."

She hesitated.

Lincoln exhaled and began rubbing the oil into her skin. "Remember when I told you there was something I needed to tell you?"

"The bad news?"

"I never said that it was bad news."

Of course it is. "Okay." While she waited through several of his false starts, her anxiety level began to creep up. "Just say it."

"There is something I haven't told you."

Peyton didn't like those words at all. She turned and exited the shower.

"Wait. Where are you going?" Lincoln followed.

She draped a towel around her body. "Nowhere. I just wanted to dry off," she lied again.

The look on his face told her that he didn't buy it. However, he didn't reach for a towel. "I'm hoping what I have to tell you isn't a big deal."

"Why don't you let me be the judge of that?" she challenged.

Lincoln suddenly felt unsure of himself. "All right. The thing is, when I first met you in New York I had no idea who you were."

She blinked. "O-okay."

"But when we went on our first date, I did put two and two together."

"Linc," she said, clutching her hands. "Will you just spill it? You're making me a nervous wreck."

"I'm friends with your brother," he blurted out. "I know I should have said something sooner, but when you told me that you wouldn't date another friend of his, I clammed up."

Peyton stared at him.

He exhaled. "I didn't tell Flex either. He, sort of, made the same comment about it being a no-no. For the last three months it's been killing me not to tell you."

Lincoln waited for her to say something and was surprised when she suddenly burst out laughing.

Chapter 27

"That's it?" Peyton wiped tears from her eyes as she continued to laugh. "That's your big news? I thought you were about to tell me that you were *gay* or something."

Lincoln winced and then joined her in her laughter.

She caught her breath and sat on the bed. "Well, I do remember my telling you all my horror stories dealing with Flex's friends, so I can see why you were hesitant in bringing it up."

"Oh, thank goodness." He relaxed. "You have no idea what a relief it is to hear you say that." He crossed the room and pulled her into his arms.

Her laughter quieted down as she slumped into his embrace. "Don't ever scare me like that again."

"I'll try not to." He kissed her and wondered whether he should tell her about today's events, but he wasn't entirely comfortable telling her that Flex had lied to them. Flex should be the one to straighten that out.

"Is there anything else I should know?" she asked, staring bright-eyed at him.

He hesitated. "I don't have any secrets, but . . . I

think we need to talk to your brother tomorrow. I think there's something he wants to tell you."

She stiffened. "Has something happened?"

"No. Nothing like that." He kissed her, then changed the subject. "Do you know what I could go for right about now?"

"What's that?"

"Pizza!" He stood up and swept her up into his arms. "I'm starving."

"Good. That makes two of us."

He carried her into the living room where they ate cold pizza and drank warm wine. By the time the sun rose, the lovers returned to bed and fell into a deep slumber while cocooned in each other's arms.

Flex took his time going downstairs for breakfast. He spent the night memorizing a speech and preparing for the consequences of his actions. When he reached the kitchen, he was just in time to greet Michael's fiancé, Phil, as he was heading out to work.

Two days before the man's wedding and still he had his nose to the grindstone.

"Heard about last night," Phil said, grabbing his suit jacket. "One of these days, we're going to have to try and rein in the Adams women.

"Good luck," Marlin said, descending the staircase. "I gave up trying to get their mother under control early on."

Phil laughed and shook his head as he slipped out the front door.

Marlin looked to his son. "He'll learn sooner or later."

Flex smiled. "If he hasn't learned by now, then I don't hold out too much hope for him." He turned back toward the kitchen. "Would you like some coffee?"

"Don't mind if I do."

Father and son shuffled into the kitchen with awkward smiles.

"I'm surprised Mike isn't up," Marlin commented. He reached for his beloved raisin bran cereal. "Then again, nosing in other folks' business is pretty tiring work."

Flex cracked another smile. Everything in his childhood home was where it always was. The coffee and filters were in the second cabinet from the stove and the box of Equal was in the cupboard above the refrigerator.

"So, where's your friend?" Marlin asked suddenly. "Did you two get a good night's sleep?"

"Actually, Trey didn't stay here last night, Pop."

"You two fighting again?"

Flex glanced over at his dad and read genuine concern in his expression. It was time. Maybe trying his speech out on his dad wouldn't be so bad. "The only reason Trey and I had an argument was that he found out I lied to you guys."

"Lied about what?" Michael's voice whipped from across the kitchen.

Flex looked up. For a fleeting moment, he thought about backing out of this, but knew that if he didn't clear this up, Lincoln would.

He took a deep breath and spilled the beans. "Trey is not and has never been my boyfriend. I lied about the whole thing."

After only a few hours of sleep, Peyton opened her eyes to the sound of birds, chirping outside her bedroom window. Instead of attempting to get out of bed, she snuggled closer to the hard body lying next to her. For a long time, she just lay there listening to the sound of his heartbeat and the steady flow of his breathing pattern.

This was the happiest she'd ever been; plus, she'd never felt this comfortable with a man.

Absently, she ran a finger down the open span of his chest, and before she knew it she was drawing invisible heart shapes and signing her name.

"I see you're awake," Lincoln said. His deep baritone held a rough edge this early in the morning.

"Yeah." She stretched her neck and planted a kiss against his chin. "We have a lot to do before we meet my sisters."

"You mean we have to get out of bed?"

"Can you believe it?"

Lincoln moaned. "I can see now that this is going to be a sleep-deprivation type of vacation."

"You had plenty of chances to sleep last night."

"And miss out on all that good lovin'? No way." He curled toward her and stole a kiss.

With her head swimming with delight, Peyton wanted to shirk her responsibilities and lie in bed all day with the man of her dreams. But the thought of Michael doing her bodily harm if she didn't pick up the rest of those wedding decorations was enough for her to fling back the sheets.

"We better get up."

Lincoln groaned. "Do we have to?"

"I'm afraid so."

After a few more minutes of whining and complaining, Lincoln finally got out of bed and joined her for another shower. While they were busy lathering each other up, Peyton heard her phone ringing in the distance, but was in no hurry to run and answer it.

They played with each other more than they bathed, and after an hour of such shenanigans, they left the bathroom and rushed to get ready for their day.

"We're going to have to stop somewhere and buy you some clothes," Peyton said, after watching him pout about the clothes he had worn the day before.

"That's all right. I'm sure I'll be picking up my luggage today."

"You must have better confidence in the airlines than I do."

Lincoln laughed. "Nothing as serious as that."

"Well, are you ready to go?" she asked.

"What, no breakfast?"

Peyton wiggled her feet into a pair of sandals and then grabbed her purse. "We're going to have to pick up something along the way. I also have another surprise for you today." She winked.

Lincoln's lips sloped unevenly. "I have a feeling today is going to be a day full of surprises."

After Flex's announcement, Michael called Frankie, who then called Sheldon, who then called Joey, and no one could reach Peyton. However, the person who seemed to have the hardest time with the confession was Marlin.

"So . . . that young man—"

"Is just a friend of mine," Flex said.

Michael couldn't stop staring and shaking her head at her brother. "I can't believe that you had me worrying about Trey all last night."

Flex winced. "I know. A part of me was still trying to avoid being found out," he confessed. "All I can say is that I'm sorry. I never meant to hurt anybody. It started because I didn't want you guys worrying about me in Georgia, and then I wanted word to get to Morgan that I had no trouble moving on. It seemed like a harmless lie."

Marlin tsked and shook his head. "No good ever

comes out of lying. I thought I raised you all up better than that."

Flex took the scolding because he deserved it.

"So what did you do, pay him to go along with this?" Michael folded her arms while the phone remained nestled under her ear.

"No. Linc . . . Trey didn't know anything until we arrived at the house. If anything, he was a good enough friend not to rat me out."

The kitchen filled with an awkward silence before Marlin, at last, cleared his throat. "Well, he was still a nice young man. Of course, now I feel a little silly for some of the things I talked to him about."

"Yeah, he told me about your talk last night," Flex said. His eyes lowered to his coffee cup. "Maybe we can go out somewhere today and talk." When his father didn't answer, Flex's gaze slid upward. "That's if you want to."

A shaky smile hugged Marlin's lips. "I think I'd like that very much."

Peyton parked outside the Couture Art Museum in the heart of downtown San Jose. She turned off the engine and turned excitedly toward Lincoln.

"This is it," she announced.

He glanced around and didn't know what to make of his surroundings. "Where are we?"

"We are at the museum that's going to host your first art show." She leaned over in her seat and kissed him. "Surprise."

She watched as astonishment sank into his features.

"You have to be joking."

"Nope." She turned and bounded out of the car. "I told Orlando, the director here, all about your work and he's just dying to work with you."

"How? When?" Lincoln followed her up toward the museum's door.

"Actually, we have thirty days to get ready for your show."

"Thirty days? Is that enough time?"

She grabbed hold of his hand. "You already have a lot pieces done. All you have to do is go home and pick out your favorite ones. We'll create a theme and presto, we'll have our first show."

Lincoln still appeared shocked as he glanced around the contemporary gallery space. "You really think I can pull this off?"

Peyton loved his bright-eyed reaction as she slid a supportive arm around his waist. "I think you're going to be fabulous."

"Ah, P.J., you came," a male's voice boomed behind them.

Peyton turned and beamed a bright smile at Orlando. "Of course, I came." She slid from Lincoln's arms and into the friendly director's. "I also brought you my latest protégé."

"Ah." Orlando stretched out a hand toward Lincoln. "I heard a lot about your work, Mr. Carver. I'm sure we'll work beautifully together."

Lincoln pumped his hand, while his smiled beamed from ear to ear. "I can't tell you how thrilled I am about this opportunity."

"All I can say is, if you're half as good as P.J. claims, I have the feeling that this is going to be the beginning of a beautiful relationship."

Flex was a nervous wreck when he arrived at the Peppermill later that day for lunch, but he was determined to finally gain closure. As difficult as it was to confess to his family, he was certain it was nothing compared to the humiliation he was about to feel once he talked to Morgan.

There was no excuse for Flex's behavior in the past twenty-four hours. In fact, he wanted to chalk the whole thing up to temporary insanity. Thank goodness he had a true friend in Lincoln Carver. Granted, he was upset about Flex's whopper of a story, but he didn't judge or end their friendship. Heck, had it not been for Lincoln, Flex would have spent this entire trip avoiding his father, but now he was more than hopeful they could repair the damage they'd inflicted on each other a year ago.

Peyton had found herself a good man in Lincoln. He just hoped she knew it.

Flex followed his hostess through the Peppermill's dark maze to an empty table near the back. "Thank you," he said, taking his seat.

Once he was alone, he practiced the speech he'd prepared during his ride over. But out of his list of questions, only one was important: why did he leave?

Ten years was a long time to spend with someone you thought you knew, someone you thought you loved, and someone you thought loved you.

Minutes into his rehearsed speech, Flex noticed the hostess heading back toward him. He straightened and put on his best smile before he noticed Morgan brought a guest.

"Flex. I'm so happy you made it," Morgan greeted him, extending a cold hand. "I hope you don't mind, but I took the liberty to invite Vince. We're, uh, sort of seeing each other."

Vince stretched out his hand.

Flex felt sick as he accepted it.

Morgan glanced around. "So, where's Trey?"

Chapter 28

"You're going to love this place," Peyton bragged. "My sisters and I come here all the time."

Lincoln opened the door of the Peppermill. "As long as they serve food, they're all right with me," he joked, and followed her inside.

The restaurant's darkness jarred Lincoln, but once his vision adjusted, he was quite impressed with the place's ambience.

The smiling hostess finally approached her podium. "Oh, hello, P.J. Are you meeting your sisters today?"

"Not today, Didi. I'm, uh, bringing in a new customer." She winked.

Didi's gaze scanned Lincoln as she gave him a flirtatious smile. "I sure hope he's going to be a regular."

Lincoln smiled broadly. "You never know."

The young hostess blushed and grabbed two menus from behind the podium. "Follow me."

Lincoln and Peyton laced their hands together and then fell in step behind Didi.

They were led to a circular table with a fire crackling in the center gas firepit. "This is different."

"Do you like?" Peyton asked, sliding into her chair.

"Love it. Now, let's see if we can put some food in our bellies."

"A man with a one-track mind."

"Don't try to front. I heard your stomach growling in the car."

Peyton blushed. "Oh, you heard that?"

"Uh-huh. You know, I seem to remember you telling me that you knew how to use a stove."

"I do."

Lincoln rolled his eyes. "So you say. Pizza for dinner, and no breakfast. It's not looking too good."

Her mouth fell open. "I've been . . . It's not my fault that we . . ."

"Well, there's six more days left in my vacation." He shrugged. "Who knows? I just might get a chance to taste these fictitious culinary skills."

"Fictitious?" She popped his hand. "All right. We're not going to my father's today. I'm inviting everyone over to my place. You're going to get a home-cooked meal."

Laughing, Lincoln held up his hands. "Hey, I don't want to put you out. If you can't cook, you can't cook. It won't change the way I feel about you."

"I *can* cook. You'll see. I'm going to make a big meal. You'll eat it and you'll like it."

"All right, all right. I believe you."

"Speaking of which, I seem to remember you bragging about being handy around the house."

The corners of Lincoln's lips curled wickedly. "I thought I was very handy last night." Despite the low lighting, Lincoln watched as Peyton's face darkened with embarrassment.

"I guess I walked into that one," she said.

"I'm afraid so." He winked, and then leaned forward to take her hand. "For the hundredth time, thank you for arranging this show. I can't tell you how much it means to me."

"I'm just doing what a good agent is supposed to do." She winked back.

His eyes widened in surprise, and a cocky grin hooked the corners of Lincoln's mouth. "Does this mean what I think it does?"

"Hey." She shrugged. "I always said I could separate business from pleasure. Now I get the chance to prove it."

"This day just keeps getting better and better." He lifted her hand and brought it to his lips. "I wonder what the night will be like."

"You'll just have to wait and see." Her blush darkened.

"And on that note," he said, scooting out of the booth, "I think I'll head to the men's room."

She turned in her seat and pointed toward the back of the restaurant. "Just go around the bar. You can't miss it."

Lincoln lifted her hand and brushed a kiss against her knuckles. "I'll be right back." He stood and followed her instructions. When he reached the bar, a voice boomed at him.

"There he is! Trey, over here!"

Lincoln's head jerked at the sound of his name. To his right, he spotted someone waving. "Me?" He glanced around to make sure the person was referring to him, and then jabbed a thumb to center of his chest for a double check.

"Yes, you," the man said.

Frowning, he headed toward the stranger. Just as he was certain the man had mistaken him for someone else, recognition surged through his brain. "Morgan," he said, with a jolt of surprise.

Morgan extended his hand. "Flex was just telling us that you couldn't make it."

Lincoln's gaze fell to the two men settled around the dark table. He immediately recognized Flex's large physique, despite his head being cradled in his hands. "Did he now?"

"Oh, where are my manners?" Morgan said. "I'd like to introduce the new man in my life, Vince Mackey. Vince, this is Flex's new hunk, Trey Carver."

"Nice to meet you," Vince said, jutting out his hand.

Lincoln's emotions rocketed from annoyance to anger faster than the speed of light. His *buddy* had promised to clear this up, but apparently he hadn't.

"Here. Won't you sit down?" Morgan asked.

Flex still refused to meet Lincoln's gaze, but there was something about his slumped body language that weakened Lincoln's anger. Memories of Flex saving his life flashed through Lincoln's mind, and he couldn't bring himself to expose his friend in a lie.

"Trey?" Morgan asked, frowning.

"Yes?" Lincoln turned his attention toward Morgan.

"Are you going to join us?"

Lincoln cast a glance across the restaurant to where he'd left Peyton. Maybe he could spare just a few minutes. "Sure," he said, flashing a smile.

Flex lifted his head. His surprised gaze finally met Lincoln's.

"But I was just on my way to the bathroom," Lincoln hinted.

Flex stood. "I'll come with you." He flashed the other men a shaky smile. "We'll be right back."

Lincoln turned and led Flex toward the back of the restaurant. However, the moment they entered the men's room, Lincoln rounded on him. "You've lost your mind!"

"I kept my word," Flex said defensively. "I told my family the truth first thing this morning."

"Then what the heck was that out there?"

Flex's shoulders slumped as his explanation spilled

forth. "Look, the past year hasn't been easy for me—emotionally, anyway. Maybe I did hightail it out of California to get away from my problems. I came here for a real heart-to-heart with Morgan, but he showed up with this new guy and—" He stopped. "I was going to tell him the truth, honestly."

Lincoln's anger dissolved at the genuine look of emotional turmoil on his friend's face. "I guess relationships are complicated no matter who's involved, huh?"

Flex exhaled a long, tired breath. "Well, at least now you know I'm a fraud. I don't have all the answers when it comes to relationships. I can't manage my own love life."

Lincoln diverted his gaze from his friend's pained expression. "You're right. This isn't the Flex I know. You would have told me that honesty was the best policy and to lay all my cards out on the table."

Flex sighed.

"Fortunately for you, I'm not going to give you that same ridiculous advice. If you go out there with your tail tucked between your legs, you might as well paint the word *loser* on your forehead. Tell you what, I'm going to help you out," he decided. "This, uh, Morgan dude pulled a fast one on you, right?"

"Look, Linc, you don't have to. This is my mess. I'll figure something out."

Lincoln tossed up his hands. "Have it your way. Go out there and tell Morgan and his *new friend* the truth."

Flex hedged.

Lincoln paced around. "Why would Morgan bring that guy here if not to rub it in your face?"

"Maybe he thought I was bringing you?"

"Nah, not after the way I left last night. I'll tell you why: he's still trying to pull your strings. He saw how you froze up last night. Hell, a blind man could have seen that."

"I forget, are you supposed to be helping?"

"Of course I am." Lincoln slapped a hand across his back. "But you have to toughen up. Morgan came here to play mind games, and we're not going to let him win."

"We're not?"

"Hell no. Morgan has to know he can still get you. And that could only mean one thing."

"What?"

Lincoln announced the obvious answer. "He wants you back,"

Flex blinked. "You really think so?"

Lincoln slowed his pep talk to study him. "The question is whether you want him back."

A toilet flushed and both men turned as a stall door swung open.

A pencil-thin Caucasian in office blues emerged and glanced nervously at them.

At six-four and six-three, Flex and Lincoln towered over the skittish man as he rushed to wash and dry his hands.

"Excuse me," he said, edging around them to get out the door.

Lincoln's gaze returned to Flex and the two men burst out laughing.

Flex walked over to the sink and began washing his hands.

Lincoln studied him. "You know you didn't answer my question. Do you want to get back with this dude?"

"Not on your life."

Lincoln pounded his friend on the back. "This guy messes with a friend of mine, then he's messing with me."

"That's nice of you, Linc, but—"

"C'mon. We can do this. We'll just put on a little show for him—make him jealous." He headed toward the door, and then stopped. "Problem." He turned toward back to face Flex. "Peyton is also out there, too. You haven't told her the truth yet, have you?"

"I haven't had a chance, but surely the sisters' network has caught up with her by now."

Lincoln shook his head. "No, she doesn't know. We have to talk to her first."

"Okay."

Lincoln nodded and drew a deep breath. "And another thing. What happens here at the Peppermill—"

"Stays at the Peppermill," Flex finished for him. "Got it."

The men waltzed out the restroom confident in their new agenda. However, getting away from Morgan and Vince wasn't such an easy feat.

"Wait, where are you two going?" Morgan asked, jumping to his feet. "The waitress has been by twice asking for your drink order."

Lincoln tensed when Flex draped an arm around his shoulder.

"Ah, Trey told me he hitched a ride with my sister, so I just want to go by her table and say hi."

"You mean Peyton?" Morgan asked.

"Uh, yeah," Lincoln said, frowning. "Why, did you see her?"

"Yep. She just passed by here a few minutes ago on her way to the restroom. I told her you two were here. She said that she'd stop by when she came out."

Vince tugged Morgan's arm. "I thought she said she hadn't had the chance to meet Trey yet."

Morgan's brows furrowed in thought. "Maybe we

misunderstood her." He gestured to the empty chairs in front of him. "Anyway, have a seat."

Lincoln tossed a worried look over his shoulder. "Guys?"

Flex's arm fell from Lincoln's shoulder.

"Oh, here she comes now." Morgan's chair screeched as he stood up and called, "Peyton. Peyton. Over here."

Neither Lincoln nor Flex turned around, but at the sound of her scandals clicking against the floor, Lincoln felt sick.

"There's my baby brother." She rushed up into her brother's arms. "I'm so sorry I didn't get a chance to see you last night." She squeezed him tight and kissed his cheek. "I'm so happy you're home."

"P.J., there's something I have to tell you," Flex began.

"There you are." Peyton slid out of his arms and cast her eyes toward Lincoln. "I was wondering what was taking you so long." She moved from her brother to Lincoln.

Lincoln tried to pull her away. "I need to talk to you for a minute."

"I'm confused here," Morgan said, easing closer. "Peyton, I thought you said that you hadn't met Flex's new boyfriend?"

She perked up and looked around. "I haven't. Where is he?"

Lincoln and Flex tried again. "Peyton—"

Morgan crossed his arms. "What are you talking about? You have your arms around Trey right now."

Chapter 29

"What are you talking about? This is *my* boyfriend." Peyton laughed, and then glanced up at a frowning Lincoln.

His arms tightened around her. "Peyton, we need to talk."

He tried to lead her away, but she instantly sensed something was amiss and refused to budge. "Talk about what?"

"Yeah? This I'd like to hear, too," Morgan said, crossing his arms.

"Wait." Flex huffed out a breath. "I have something to say."

"Flex." Lincoln gave him a strained look, while he continued to tug Peyton.

"Oh . . . my . . . God!" Peyton's eyes rounded with disbelief, a wave of panic seizing her as the entire restaurant began to spin.

Morgan chuckled. "It looks like someone is playing both sides of the fence."

Vince snickered. "At least he's keeping it in the family."

"Oh . . . my . . . God," she exclaimed again, jerking from Lincoln's grasp. "You're Trey?"

"Yes, my name is Trey, but—"

"Oh my God!"

"It's not what you think," Lincoln and Flex said simultaneously.

Peyton kept backing up, shaking her head. Finally, the bomb had dropped. She had finally discovered what was wrong with her perfect man—he was . . . on the down low.

Michael's words roared in her head. *"You'd be surprised how many men swing both ways."* Her voice was quickly replaced by Lincoln's earlier confession. *"I'm a friend of your brother's."*

"I think I'm going to be sick." She bolted from the small crowd.

Both Lincoln and Flex reached for her in a few quick strides.

"Don't touch me!"

"P.J. Listen to me," Flex said. "I—"

"I'm going to be sick!" She pushed her way between them.

"Peyton," Lincoln shouted and once again caught up with her in two long strides to block her exit. "Why won't you listen? I'm *not* Flex's—" His head jerked back from the hard blow of her hand.

"I wish I'd never laid eyes on you," she seethed. Pain consumed her heart and she was possessed with the need to retaliate. "You disgust me!"

An unfamiliar male voice interrupted them. "Excuse me, I'm the manager on duty. I'm afraid I'm going to have to ask you two to leave."

"Gladly," she said, lifting her chin and meeting Lincoln's angry glare. "I never want to see you again."

From over his shoulder she saw her brother now move toward her, but she quickly turned and headed out of the restaurant. And then something akin to an iron vise fastened around her waist and lifted her off her feet.

"You're going to listen to me whether you want to or not," Lincoln said in a low growl.

Peyton's anger morphed to pure shock over the fact that she was being manhandled. "Put me down!"

When Lincoln shoved open the glass door, the couple was instantly drenched in sunlight. They received a few stares from people heading into the restaurant, but neither Lincoln nor Peyton cared.

"Put me down," she demanded again, and was stunned when her feet unceremoniously hit the concrete. Her knees buckled, but she was saved when Lincoln's strong hands steadied her.

"What is wrong with you?" he growled.

"Me?" she thundered back.

"I'm not your brother's boyfriend!" His features hardened into stone. "How could you even think that? You believe me to be so low that I would be having an affair with both of you? I don't even know what to say to that."

Peyton's ready retort dissolved on the tip of her tongue. For several heartbeats, she could only manage to blink at him.

"I thought that you knew me. I thought you knew my heart."

His words crushed her soul.

"It's true," Flex said softly.

Her gaze shot over to her brother.

"That's what we've been trying to tell you," he added.

She stepped back and stared at the two men, while a gamut of emotions warred within her. "So . . . you're not Trey?"

Lincoln turned to Flex angrily. "Why don't you explain?"

Flex nodded and stepped forward. "P.J., you first have to know that I never meant to hurt you."

"Is he or is he not *your* Trey?"

"Yes *and* no."

Peyton's head threatened to explode. "C'mon. Give me something. I'm starting to feel like the butt of a bad joke."

"I lied, P.J.," Flex finally blurted. "I lied to you about Trey—Lincoln. I wanted word to get back to Morgan that I'd moved on and I used the first name that popped into my head. Lincoln had no idea about any of this until yesterday. He was willing to play along in there to help me save face in front of Morgan."

"What?" She shook her head. This was all too much information to take in at one time. Her boyfriend was her brother's boyfriend and now he wasn't. It was as if they were purposely trying to drive her insane.

"That doesn't make sense. Why would you lie about something like that—and why with him?"

"Because I thought he was someone my family would never meet," Flex reasoned. "It's stupid, I know. You have to believe me. Lincoln didn't know anything about my lying to my family until yesterday. His willingness to lie to Morgan was nothing more than him trying to help a friend."

Peyton stared at her brother in outrage, but when her gaze swung to Lincoln, humiliation rose and clogged her throat. "So you're not on the down low?"

His features twisted in confusion. "The what?"

At long last, she released a relieved breath. She even tried to laugh at herself and the situation, but her voice shattered like glass. When she took a tentative step forward, Lincoln's hard gaze smote her where she stood.

Flex turned his attention toward his friend as well. "This isn't her fault."

Lincoln gave him a small nod, but his gaze was now infused with hurt.

Peyton couldn't shake the feeling of being the prosecutor and the defendant. She was at a loss as to how to repair the damage her harsh words had created. The only thing she could think to say was, "Seems like I owe you an apology."

Another slow nod.

"Given the circumstances, you can't blame me for—"

"Not listening?" he supplied for her. "Automatically thinking the worst of me?"

Flex step forward. "Linc—"

"Do you mind leaving us alone for a few minutes?" Lincoln's hard gaze swung to Flex.

Flex folded his meaty arms as if he was going to refuse the request. But when Peyton laid a hand against his shoulder, he quickly acquiesced.

Peyton watched her brother's reluctance as he turned and walked away. A couple exited the Peppermill and cast their curious gazes in their direction. "Do you mind if we could at least go somewhere where we have a little more privacy?"

She pretended her heart didn't break at his hesitancy, just as she pretended she was drowning in an ocean of shame. Neither spoke as they walked toward her car and even long after they had settled into their seats.

"I'm sorry," she, at last, said with a shrug. "There's nothing else I can say. I should have given you more time to explain, *but* I was duped in this whole thing."

"I know." He glanced out of his side window. He seemed determined to end the conversation before it ever got started.

After the long seconds stretched into minutes, he glanced over at her. "Is it always going to be like this between us?"

She frowned at the question.

"*You* waiting for the bubble to burst, the shoe to fall—this whole 'when is this man going to turn into a frog?' thing you have going here."

Peyton opened her mouth, but when she realized that she didn't have a ready answer, she closed it again.

Disappointment etched into Lincoln's features. "You know, as long as I can remember I just wanted to understand women. And now I think I understand *you* all too well."

Though she feared his next words, she lifted her chin high as she met his gaze.

"It seems like you just won't let go of old baggage." His words softened as he held her gaze. "Not every man wants to use or hurt you. And as much as I want to be your prince, I fear the day you truly discover I'm not perfect. My faults will just be added to a growing list of things you can't stand about men."

"I don't know about that. This time it was my brother who lied to me."

"And yet you wouldn't give him the opportunity to explain either."

Peyton knew that she should be defending herself. She was, after all, a product of her past relationships, but the line blurred between what were lessons learned and what was considered baggage. "So what are you trying to say?"

He lowered his gaze. "I want to end this. I don't think we have what it takes to make this relationship work."

Chapter 30

The wedding

"He doesn't think you have what it takes to make the relationship work?" Michael repeated, pacing back and forth in her wedding gown. "He actually said that?"

Joey tossed up her hands. "Will you please be still? I'm trying to fasten your dress."

Michael rolled her eyes and forced herself to stand still, but her foot tapped nonstop against the floor.

Frankie turned her soured expression toward Peyton. "So what did you say?"

Peyton shrugged as her gaze fell to a patch of her blush-pink gown. "What could I say?"

Her sisters waited for her to continue, but the sad fact was there was nothing else to tell them.

"Don't tell me you just sat there," Michael said in astonishment. "You were just telling us that you thought that he was *the one.*"

"Mike, be still," Joey barked.

Peyton swallowed the rising lump in her throat

and fought back the threat of tears. "I've been wrong before."

Frankie settled a hand against her shoulder. "Are you going to be all right?"

"Aren't I always?" Peyton forced her chin up and ran through a short list of affirmations, but they were all crap and she knew it.

"You know, this is all Francis's fault," Michael started up again. "None of this would have happened if he'd just been honest."

"It's not his fault." Peyton shook her head as she stood up. "Lincoln said that I have too much baggage and severe trust issues."

The room fell silent.

She glanced back at her sisters. Their gazes darted around the room.

"What? Don't tell me that you agree with him?"

"Well," Joey began, but quickly clamped her mouth shut when Michael elbowed her.

Peyton rounded on her sisters. "You have to be kidding me. All of you feel this way?"

Everyone's eyes continued to avoid Peyton's.

"Okay. So I might be a little selective or even picky when it comes to men, but that doesn't mean I have baggage. Baggage is having umpteen children—each one having a different daddy. That's not me. I'm a successful, if I do say so myself, independent woman—"

"Maybe too independent," Sheldon chimed in from across the room. She shrugged when everyone's gaze swung in her direction, and then reclined back against the chaise with her belly protruding outward. "Well, if she has to hear the truth, it might as well be from us."

Peyton's gaze slid back to Michael, Frankie, and Joey. "Well?"

Her sisters' evasive eyes finally met in her direction, while a collective sigh filled the room.

Peyton's heart sank at the sight of gloom and doom painted on their faces. "Just forget it." She waved them off and turned away. Their failure to back her up on this issue felt like a knife to the heart, and it was difficult to pretend otherwise.

"C'mon, P.J.," Sheldon said. "Would you rather we lie? You *can* be a little hard on men. We've told you this before."

Peyton clenched her jaw and squeezed her eyes shut. Had the iron fence around her heart cost her the best thing that had come into her life?

She flinched when a pair of cool hands settled on her shoulders, but then relaxed when Frankie's comforting voice brushed against her ear. "We all understand why. It's just that if you ever want to be in a meaningful relationship again, you're going to have to risk having your heart broken."

"I already have." Peyton opened her eyes, but her vision was blurred by brimming tears. She drew in a shaky breath and winced as if her heart were being torn from her chest. "And it hurts like hell."

She turned toward Frankie and instantly wrapped her arms around her. "I really did screw this up, didn't I?"

"Oh, P.J." Frankie squeezed her tight.

Before Peyton knew it, two more sets of arms enveloped her. She was nearly crushed beneath the wave of love and support.

"P.J., you're going to have to forgive me," Sheldon said from the chaise. "But I don't think I'm going to be able to get up."

The statement elicited a chorus of laughter from the sisters.

From this moment, Peyton drew a measure of comfort from her sisters. Yet she still wished like hell there was some way she could get her man back.

* * *

It was a beautiful day for an outside wedding. As friends and family filled every chair on the lush lawn, there was no mistaking the buzz of excitement. After years of being engaged, Michael and Phil were finally getting married. Many had doubted this day would ever come.

A hush fell over the crowd as "The Wedding March" suddenly filled the air. Tears sprang to Peyton's eyes as she took her position to march single file out onto lawn. It was all she could do to concentrate on placing one foot in front of the other. Once she reached her marked area, she was to link arms with her groomsman partner, but way before she hit that mark, her gaze zeroed in on the man approaching her.

"Lincoln . . . ?" Her steps faltered and she quickly hustled to get back into step with the music.

She hit her mark and paused again, when Lincoln, handsome in a black and white tuxedo, offered her his arm.

"What are you doing here?"

"Filling in for a sick groomsman." He jutted his arm toward her again.

Disappointment crushed her heart.

"And of course, I wanted to try and win you back."

Someone coughed and jarred Peyton back to reality. At last, she accepted Lincoln's arm. Together, they marched down the aisle toward the minister.

"You know, this is pretty good practice," he whispered into her ear, making her miss a step.

"You're not funny," she hissed at him. "What happened to all that stuff about us not having what it takes to make this relationship work?"

He fell silent for a couple of steps before he replied, "The thing is . . . I love you."

Tears seeped from her eyes as they finally arrived at the altar. Silently, they separated to stand at their designated positions.

Lincoln tried to calm the wild pounding of his heart. He had taken a big chance in coming there today. But he couldn't get himself to board the plane that morning. He couldn't walk out on the best thing that had ever happened to him.

He watched the rest of the wedding party as they marched down the aisle, but kept sending covetous glances toward Peyton. She was beautiful in a pink bridesmaid dress with her hair pinned up, and soft ringlets framing her face.

But Peyton refused to meet his gaze.

The wedding went off without a hitch. The crowd burst into jubilant excitement when the minister presented Mr. and Mrs. Phil Matthews.

Lincoln tolerated the silent treatment for a few minutes while everyone posed for photographs. But after that, he managed to corner Peyton before she made it to the reception tent. However, he hadn't expected to find her eyes swimming in tears.

"You know we belong together," he said gently. "I know it, too. But this is something we're going to have to work at."

She remained silent and refused to look at him.

Lincoln released a long breath. "It's up to you. Maybe you don't want to give *us* another try?"

Peyton sniffed. "It's not that," she finally said.

"Then what is it?" he asked, and then inched closer.

Wiping at a stray tear, she met his eyes. "I'm afraid that you were right yesterday. I don't know how to let go of old baggage. I don't know how not to expect the worst."

It was Lincoln's turn to lower his gaze. The silence

that stood between them made it seem as if they were attending a funeral instead of a wedding.

"But I'm willing to try. If you'd let me."

Lincoln's gaze flew back up to meet hers. Had he heard her right?

"I love you, Lincoln. I know that much." She moved closer to him. "Neither of us is perfect, but we're definitely perfect for each other. Marry me." She wrapped her arms around his neck.

He blinked in surprised. "Hey, that's my line."

"Not anymore." She smiled. "Marry me."

He rolled his eyes playfully. "I don't know. It's sort of sudden and where is my ring?"

"Going once, twice—"

"Yes," he said, and then sealed the deal with a kiss.

Cheers surrounded the couple and they immediately sprang apart.

"I guess this means I'm off the hook?" Flex asked as he draped his heavy arms around the newly engaged couple.

Peyton waved a finger in front of him. "You're not going to get off that easy."

"Guys?" Sheldon's voice sliced through the crowd. "Uh, I think I need to get to the hospital. "My water just broke."

All hell broke loose as the entire Adams clan scrambled to get Sheldon to the hospital. So much so that they had forgotten to tell her husband—who was in the bathroom. Lincoln found himself in the center of the mix, and was the appointed driver. In that instant, he was accepted as a member of the family.

A few hours later, he and Peyton stood arm in arm at the hospital's nursery. They stared and made funny faces at Sheldon's newborn baby girl.

"You know, I wouldn't mind having a few of those myself," he hinted.

"Oh? And just how many did you have in mind?" she asked, glancing up.

"One, two—a dozen."

Peyton nearly choked.

"Okay, a half dozen," he amended with a wink.

Peyton chuckled, and then slid her arms around him. "Aim . . . lower."

"Well, at least I know we'll have fun making them."

"You know, there's no crime in getting started right away."

"Sounds like a short engagement is in order."

"I think that might be best." She tilted up her chin and received a kiss. When their lips broke away, she made a confession. "I'm glad you came back."

"I'll always come back to you. I love you." He kissed her again. "So what's it going to be—Georgia or California?"

"I love you too, and I'll be happy anywhere—as long as we're together."

"California it is." He winked. "Of course, that's depending on whether my boyfriend, Flex, doesn't mind."

"Very funny." Peyton smacked him playfully on the chest. "I'm not sharing you with anyone."

Lincoln leaned down and kissed the top of her head. "Ditto."

Author's Note

I sure hope that you enjoyed reading *Measure of a Man*. Lincoln and Peyton were definitely a fun couple to write about. So much so that I doubt that this will be the last time you will read about them. Flex's five nosy sisters already have me thinking of another love story. Besides, I can't just leave Flex companionless. Stay tuned . . . I think I know just the man for Joey!

Please feel free to visit me on the Web at http://www.adriannebyrd.com.

Best of love,

Adrianne Byrd

About the Author

National best-selling author Adrianne Byrd has always preferred to live within the realms of her imagination, where all the men are gorgeous and the women are worth whatever trouble they manage to get into. As an army brat, she traveled throughout Europe and learned to appreciate and value different cultures. Now she calls Georgia home.

Her passion for writing began at the ripe old age of thirteen. It was also the age when she was introduced to romance novels by a most unlikely source: her fifteen-year-old brother. The book was probably given to keep her out of her brother's hair, but it was a gift that changed her life.

In books, Adrianne found a way out of her awkward teenage years and into a world of fictional friends that would stay with her for a lifetime. It wasn't long before her imagination took flight and she was writing her own love stories. Within a year, she completed her first book, which she vowed would never see the light of day.

Writing remained a hobby until 1994, when a coworker approached her with an article about Romance Writers of America. Who knew there was an organization of women just like her? In 1996, she sold her first novel, *Defenseless,* to Kensington Publishing.

Her first release received rave reviews from *Romantic Times* and fans. Her other novels were consistently selected as the magazine's Top Pick. In 2001, Slam Jam nominated *Say You Love Me* for best romance. Her 2003 BET release, *Comfort of a Man,* went on to win eight prestigious awards.

She has been featured in many national publications, including *Today's Black Woman, Upscale,* and *Heart and Soul.* She has also won local awards for screenwriting. In the future, she looks forward to creating characters that make people smile, laugh, and fall in love.